THE MYSTERY OF THE FALSE FINGERTIPS

JAMES HOLDING'S YOUNG ADULT MYSTERIES

The Mystery of Dolphin Inlet

The Mystery of the False Fingertips

JAMES HOLDING'S BOOKS FOR ADULTS

James Holding's Conmen & Cutthroats MEGAPACK®

James Holding's Murder & Mayhem MEGAPACK®

The Library Fuzz MEGAPACK®:
The Complete Hal Johnson Series

THE MYSTERY OF THE FALSE FINGERTIPS

JAMES HOLDING

CHAPTER 1

After Visiting Hours

Cam pulled up in front of Dutch's house about seven o'clock of a late June evening and touched the horn of his jalopy with a proprietary air. The old Chevy idled happily, a bundle of metallic vibrations and unsuspected power.

Dutch lived on the south side of town, right on the city line, in a small, somewhat isolated house. At the sound of Cam's horn he came out of the front door, letting the screen door slam behind him, and called over his shoulder, "I ought to be home by eleven, Mom. Don't wait up."

He ran down the flagstone walk to the curb and vaulted into the front seat of the jalopy beside Cam. "To the museum, my good man," he said to Cam, grinning. "Duty calls."

"Yeah," said Cam. "Night duty. They paying you time and a half for overtime? I hope?"

"Nope. No time and a half. Not like you big construction workers."

Cam laughed. "I'm just a boy with a strong back, pal, not a construction worker. If swinging a pick on a road gang puts me in shape for football in the fall, I'll be satisfied. But no night work for me. Definitely not."

"I don't mind it a bit," Dutch said. "You know something? This is the best darn summer job I've had yet. I like it."

Cam grunted, steering the jalopy nonchalantly with one hand. "But I told the girls we'd pick them up at Kathy's house about nine and buy them a coke at Cox's tonight," he protested. "Then you call and say you have to work. Where does that leave me?"

"It leaves you with two girls instead of one, you lucky dog. Take them to Cox's. You can handle two, can't you? Janet knows

I'm going to have to work nights on this job sometimes, so she won't mind. Give her my apologies, but buy her a coke, what do you say?"

"Okay," said Cam. "And we'll stop and pick you up at the museum afterward and drive you home."

"Fine." Dutch beat a rhythmic tattoo with his fingers on the ledge of the car door beside him. "Isn't it something for the girls to take summer jobs, too? Imagine Janet as a gift shop clerk at Wexler's!"

"And Kathy as a file clerk in her dad's office. That I'd like to see."

"Me, too." Dutch grinned. "You think they'll be able to last out the summer?"

"Sure. What boss would have the heart to fire such charming help?" Cam started to whistle. He turned into Pyramid Avenue where the museum and its grounds occupied a full block between Hackett and Main. "Here you are, Dutch. Portal-to-portal service. We'll be back for you about ten. All right?"

"Right. Meet you here at ten."

Cam waved a hand, put the jalopy in gear, and roared away.

"Thanks for the buggy ride," Dutch called after him.

* * * *

Dutch walked up the broad entrance steps to the museum, feeling in his pocket for his key to the employees' entrance, a small door to the left of the massive public portals, which were closed now until the museum reopened tomorrow morning at ten.

Dutch felt a secret thrill every time he realized he had a personal key to this fascinating building, that he was actually an employee of the museum.

The museum was shaped like a capital T laid on its side with the crossbar paralleling Pyramid Avenue. The cast-bronze entrance doors were in the middle of the crossbar. They gave upon a spacious, half-round lobby whose walls and floors were entirely sheathed in polished Carrara marble. Above the lobby rose a vaulted half-dome of translucent glass, supported by a semicircular row of soaring Doric columns. Directly opposite the entrance stretched the base of the T—the Egyptian wing of the museum—accessible through a high arch from the lobby. Beyond the exhibit hall were the administrative offices and workrooms. To the left of the entrance, through a similar arch, lay the museum's Grecian wing. And to the right, its Roman wing.

Dutch unlocked the small door and entered the lobby.

In a way it was like riding in a time machine, he thought. To step through that door, especially when the public was absent and a vast, echoing silence held the building in its grip, was literally like stepping from the frenetic modern world he knew into the mysterious world of the distant past. For Dutch this pleasant sensation of time travel was one of the chief reasons he liked his summer job so much.

He paused for a moment in the lobby, feeling very strongly the brooding presence of antiquity in the exhibits that filled the rooms around him. He took a deep breath, sniffing in imagination the musty air of centuries long dead. Then he laughed to himself sheepishly and said, "Boy, what a nut!" He raised his voice and called, "Tom!"

Tom Scott was the night watchman. In eighteen years Tom had never been known to miss a night's duty. During his regime nothing had ever been stolen from the museum at night; it had never even been the victim of an attempted robbery. Tom and Dutch had become fast friends during Dutch's few evenings of work since he'd started on the job two weeks ago.

"Tom!" Dutch called again.

"That you, Dutch?" Tom appeared, walking softly on his rubber soles from the shadows of the Grecian wing. "More night work?"

"Yeah. Dr. Kilty asked me if I'd finish up the Karnak labeling tonight. Anybody else here?"

Tom shook his head. "Just us. I'll be glad of your company."

"I'll be in the small workroom." Dutch pointed toward the rear of the Egyptian wing. "When you make your rounds back there, don't shoot when you see the light. Okay? It'll only be me." He laughed.

"Okay," Tom said comfortably. "Long as I know you're there. Ain't even dark yet, Dutch. I won't be bothering you for a spell. Don't let the mummies get you, though." Tom had never quite overcome his own superstitious uneasiness in the presence of the several mummies of the Egyptian collection.

"Don't worry"—Dutch grinned at him—"no four-thousand-year-old mummy's going to bother me tonight. I'll be too busy."

He walked through the long, exhibit-cluttered Egyptian Hall, heading for the workrooms at the rear of the building. Only a few small windows, far up against the hall's ceiling line, admitted daylight to the enormous room. It was illuminated during visiting hours by concealed fluorescent lights, now switched off for the night. Even Tom's small night light was not yet turned on. Outdoors it was still broad daylight; in here the shadows had begun to gather thickly.

They gathered around the colossal figure of Ramses II, powerful king of the Egyptians in the thirteenth century B.C., now seated in half-size replica against the museum wall. Even half size, this reproduction of one of the four huge figures guarding the entrance to the Temple of Abou-Simbel in Nubia was still over thirty feet tall. Beside it loomed a statue of beaked and feathered Horus, hawk-god of ancient Egypt. And across the hall, already fading into the evening darkness, a reproduction of the Alabaster Sphinx of Memphis regarded Dutch with inscrutable gaze.

Dutch lifted a hand and said, "Hi, fellows," in a friendly voice to this shadowy trio as he passed into a narrow corridor at the end of Egyptian Hall and followed it around to the back of the administration offices. There he entered a small workroom and switched on the light over a work table. On the table a typewriter, a stack of exhibit cards, a sketch of the museum's scale model of the Temple of Karnak, and a number of handwritten captions were spread out, just as Dutch had left them when he went home to dinner at five o'clock.

With a sigh of contentment he settled down to check the new exhibit captions against the sketch for the last time before he typed them and sent them to the job printer who would run off the finished cards.

* * * *

He worked steadily, losing track of time and place as the world darkened outside the museum and he was caught up in the world of ancient Thebes. Great Hypostyle Hall, The Avenue of Ram-Headed Sphinxes, Festival Hall, The Temple of Amen-Ra—the very names he worked with were his passports to the magic past.

He was oblivious to all else. Beyond the administration offices and workrooms Egyptian Hall slept as silently as an undiscovered tomb in the Valley of the Kings.

About nine o'clock Dutch began to type his captions, his typewriter making a cheerful clatter against the quiet of the museum. Once, at what time Dutch couldn't say, Tom stuck his head in the workroom door and said, "All quiet on the Egyptian front, Dutch. Want a cup of coffee?"

Mechanically Dutch said, "No, thanks, Tom. I'm almost finished now." And Tom went away on his rubber soles.

At 9:45 Dutch began to gather his typed captions together. He stood up and stretched to get the kinks out of his back, stiff from bending over the typewriter. Better clean up and get ready to go home, he thought. Cam and the girls would stop for him in a few minutes now. He was tired. It had been a long day.

He was reaching for an envelope in which to stow his typed captions when he heard the thump.

It came only once and it wasn't loud. What could it be—a strange noise like that? And where did it come from?

From the Egyptian wing of the museum, Dutch told himself. Where else? If it had come from the Roman or Grecian wings, or from outside the museum, he couldn't have heard it. Not in this central workroom. So it had to come from Egyptian Hall. Dutch thought to himself, let's have a look. Maybe old Tom has tripped over a mummy case.

He left the light on in the workroom to guide him through the first leg of the corridor that ended at the doorway into the Egyptian wing. Reaching this doorway, he stopped momentarily, his gaze ranging down the vast Egyptian Hall. It was completely dark, a cavern of blackness to his light-accustomed eyes. Something didn't seem quite right about that to Dutch.

In a moment he figured out what it was. The Egyptian wing shouldn't be in total darkness at this hour. Tom's single night light should be burning halfway down the left-hand wall toward the lobby entrance. It gave only enough light to help Tom see where he was going as he made his rounds. That single bulb would have been clearly visible from where Dutch was standing.

But it wasn't burning now.

Puzzled, Dutch took a soft step into Egyptian Hall.

At that moment the sharp beam of a flashlight cut the darkness. It came from a spot about halfway down the room and toward the center aisle. Dutch nodded to himself. Sure, he thought, relieved, Tom's night light has burned out, so he's using his flash.

"Tom," he called out, "is that you?"

The flashlight winked out like a snuffed candle. There was no answer.

"Tom?" Dutch tried again. He felt a slight shiver of uneasiness slide down between his shoulder blades "Tom! Anything wrong?"

No answer.

Dutch took a hesitant step forward. Unexpectedly then, the flashlight snapped on again. The beginnings of real fright made Dutch's leg muscles quiver. He raised his voice to call out more loudly than before, thinking that perhaps Tom hadn't heard him. But with his mouth open to speak, he suddenly smothered the words. Because just then the flashlight beam moved in a short arc laterally across the hall, steadily and deliberately, and finally settled and held on a certain spot on the floor of the central aisle.

Dutch was some yards away from the circle of light on the floor. But he was close enough to see plainly what it disclosed.

It was a man's head. Resting on the cold marble of the museum floor. Dutch could not see the body below the head. It disappeared into the blackness outside the lighted circle. There was a small, dark, wet stain visible on the white forehead—Tom's forehead. For it was Tom who was lying there in the flashlight's beam.

"Tom!" Dutch yelled then, galvanized, everything forgotten but the fact that his friend Tom seemed to be hurt. "What's the matter, Tom?"

Had he fainted? Had a heart attack? Maybe tripped over a mummy case and knocked himself out?

While these swift speculations raced through his mind, Dutch himself was racing at full running stride down the marble aisle of the Egyptian wing. In his anxiety about his friend, Dutch did not think to ask himself a very important question: If Tom was lying there unconscious, who was holding that flashlight?

This didn't occur to him until a moment later. Until, in fact, he neared the circle of light and made out a squat silhouette behind the flashlight. Until he reached Tom's body, began to stoop toward it, and suddenly caught from the corner of his eye a blur of movement in the shadow of a mummy case behind him. Until that blur of movement terrifyingly resolved itself into a hunched mummy-like figure with one arm lifted, springing toward him. Until something crashed into Dutch's head just under his ear with a sickening, numbing crunch that sent him diving down into nothingness.

CHAPTER 2

Mystery at the Museum

It was two minutes to ten when Cam pulled up outside the museum and switched off the motor of his Chevy. Kathy and Janet were in the front seat with him.

"He's not here," Cam said. "Must still be working." He checked his watch. "We're a couple of minutes early. Relax, girls." He found some rock-and-roll music on the miniature transistor radio in his shirt pocket, tuned it down low, and leaned back in the seat.

"Dutch does work awfully hard," said Janet, a faint note of pride in her voice. "He takes this museum job very seriously. He's really interested in it." Her pale blond hair glinted in the glow of a nearby streetlight as she moved her head. She laughed. "I wish I could get as enthusiastic about clerking in Wexler's Gift Shop as Dutch is about cataloguing ancient Egyptians. I'd own the store in no time!"

Janet was a forthright, quick-witted girl with delicate, pixie-like features and a petite figure. She seemed far too small, somehow, to contain the abundance of high spirits and fierce loyalties she brought to living. Her violet eyes were alert behind horn-rimmed glasses. She laughingly explained the glasses were essential because she was 20-20-20—that is, she had twenty-twenty vision up to twenty inches. Beyond that, she couldn't tell her friends from her enemies, she said. Yet her spectacles gave her vivacious face a studious cast that added to her appeal. At least Dutch thought so. He described Janet as "Nefertiti with glasses," which pleased Janet greatly when she found out who Nefertiti was and saw from pictures of the famous Egyptian queen how truly beautiful she had been.

"I think," Cam said lazily, "that our hard-working friend Dutch is bucking for the curator's job. Whoo! He can have his dusty old museum. I'll stay outdoors in the air, thanks."

Kathy turned her dark head toward Cam. She was in fact as serious-minded as Janet looked. She was built more to Cam's scale than to Janet's however, being tall, willowy, and surprisingly strong. She played on Riverlawn High's girls' basketball team, and swam the 100-meter free-style event on its swimming team. Kathy was generous, sympathetic, something of a hero worshiper (which accounted for her current admiration of Cam) and a superb dancer. She said, "I know how you feel about working outdoors, Cam, now that I'm working for Daddy in his office. Honestly, after being cooped up with a bank of filing cabinets and a computer all week, I can hardly wait for the weekend to come."

"Poor Dutch and Janet," Cam answered. "They don't even have a full weekend off."

Janet sighed in mock distress. "How true," she said. "No Saturday rest for the summer salesladies of Wexler's! Saturday is our big day. I work harder on Saturday than any other day."

"But you like it," Kathy said. "You know you do, Janet. Waiting on shoppers. Suggesting what they should buy for old Aunt Martha's birthday and everything. It's not the same when you like it."

Cam grinned. "That's the only real criticism I have of Dutch and Janet," he told Kathy darkly. "They like to work. This is a basic character flaw that will probably get them into deep trouble some day."

"Or out of it," Janet said tartly. "Isn't it ten o'clock yet?" She turned her eyes toward the museum building. "Dutch ought to be finished by now."

Kathy said, "He's late by my watch. Three minutes."

"His ancient Egyptians are really keeping him busy in there," Cam said. "I'm going to investigate." He stepped out of the jalopy. "Don't go away, ladies. Be right back."

He clicked off the radio in his pocket, went up the front walk to the museum entrance, climbed the steps and approached the employees' door. He rapped loudly on the panels.

Nothing happened. He waited a minute, then beat a tattoo on the door, put his lips close to the keyhole and called, "Hey,

Dutch! Knock it off, pal! Coffee break!" After another wait, he said through the door, "Janet's here!" But even this didn't bring any response from beyond the door.

Cam knew that door was always kept locked when the museum was closed, but driven by a growing sense of uneasiness, he reached out a hand to the knob and pushed. The door swung silently inward.

Darkness confronted him. Not even a night light was burning in the museum lobby. Nor in the Egyptian wing beyond.

"Hey, Dutch!" Cam called, full voice, into the darkness. "You still here?"

With one hand on the doorknob, he strained to hear a reply, but no sound of any kind reached him. "That's darn funny," he muttered to himself. "Where's the night watchman? Even if Dutch went home early for some reason, the guard should still be here."

No Dutch. No watchman. No lights. An unlocked front door. These four facts suddenly came together in Cam's mind. Something was wrong.

Swallowing dryly, he turned and ran back to the girls in the car. "Kathy," he said in a taut voice, "hand me the flashlight out of the glove compartment, will you please?"

She did as he asked. "Why the flashlight? What's wrong?"

"Don't know. But the museum's as black as a stack of burned toast. No sign of Dutch. And no sign of the night watchman. I'm going in and have a look. You stay here."

He turned and sped away. They could see him disappear into the employees' entrance, the flashlight beam a probing finger going before him.

Janet jumped out of the jalopy. "I'm not going to stay here!" she declared. "I'm scared. Do you suppose something's happened to Dutch? Come on, Kathy. Let's go with Cam."

Kathy joined her on the sidewalk, and they walked rapidly to the door of the museum, then paused to peer inside. They saw Cam's flashlight winking in the Egyptian Hall. "There he is," Kathy said. "Quick." They ran forward through the arch into the Egyptian wing just in time to see Cam's flashlight beam find the motionless figure of Dutch, lying in the middle of the wide aisle.

Janet screamed. Kathy breathed, "Oh, Cam, what's happened?"

And Cam, after a quick look at Dutch's white face, merely stood up and said, "Where's the telephone in this mausoleum? Anybody know?"

* * * *

At first it seemed to Dutch that somebody was pitching pennies at a line in his skull just below the right ear. Every time a penny struck the line, a big gong went "bong!" right there in his head and sent a cushiony wave of pain surging out of both ears. It was a very peculiar sensation.

Bong, bong. A penny would hit the line and go bong, and the pain pushing out of his ears didn't seem to grow any less. But it must have, because all at once he was whispering weakly, "Listen, Cam. I've got this crazy gong going off in my head, like I'm some kind of a nut…"

"Nut is right," Cam agreed, smiling down at him. "What'd you do? Run headfirst into a pyramid or something?"

The concealed fluorescents in Egyptian Hall were on now, and Dutch saw, rather mistily, that he was surrounded by Cam, Janet, and Kathy. His friends. That was fine. He grinned weakly at Janet. Then he noticed that Dr. Lynch, his family doctor, was looking down at him, too. At the doctor's side stood the uniformed figure of Police Sergeant Joe Barry. Strangest of all, Dr. Kilty, the curator of the museum, was there. And for some unaccountable reason he—Dutch—was lying on the floor, flat on his back like a mummy.

"Hey!" he said in a strong voice. He started to get to his feet. Another penny went bong in his head as it hit the lagging fine. Dr. Lynch put a hand under his arm to help him up, and Dutch suddenly got the whole picture in focus enough to begin remembering. "Tom," he said, looking anxiously around the circle of faces. "Where's Tom? The night watchman."

"He's okay, Dutch," Cam answered soothingly before anybody else could reply. "We found him over there in the aisle. He's got a little concussion, Doc Lynch says. They've carted him off to the hospital in the police ambulance. But he's okay."

"That's right," Dr. Lynch said. "How about you, Dutch? Feel pretty rocky?" He put gentle fingers on a lump behind Dutch's ear. "You took a nasty crack there. Not as nasty as Tom's, though.

You're all right, now, aren't you? No dizziness? No double vision? Just a headache?"

Dutch nodded, then stopped, wincing in pain. "How do you happen to be here, Dr. Kilty?" he asked the curator respectfully.

"This young man telephoned me," Dr. Kilty said. He looked approvingly at Cam. "He also telephoned the police and Dr. Lynch, it seems. Very quick work. We all got here within five minutes, I believe."

Cam said, "What happened, Dutch? You want us to die of suspense? I found you here on the floor when we came to drive you home. Who hit you?"

"Yeah." Sergeant Barry spoke for the first time. "You feel good enough to talk a little bit, Dutch?" Dutch had known Sergeant Barry for years, having served him many a cherry sundae from behind the counter of Cox's Dairy Store.

"Sure," said Dutch. He felt as limp as a fishing worm. He sat down carefully on the corner of a plinth that supported the crumbling capital of a papyrus column from the time of King Amenhotep III. "But I'm afraid I can't tell you very much."

"You get home to bed, Dutch," Dr. Lynch advised quietly. "You're all right, but you need a good night's rest. Why not talk tomorrow?" He picked up his black bag from the floor and started out. "I'll stop in and see Tom Scott at the hospital tomorrow."

"I'll want to talk with Tom Scott tomorrow, too, if possible," Joe Barry chimed in.

"He should be able to talk by then," Dr. Lynch said. "Good night."

"Good night," Dutch said. "And thanks for coming, Dr. Lynch."

"I'll bill Dr. Kilty." Dr. Lynch grinned and was gone.

Joe Barry hesitated, consulting Dr. Kilty with his eyes before he said to Dutch, "If you feel up to it, we'd like a quick run-down on what happened here tonight. If you make it quick, we may still be able to get a line on your head knocker…"

"Head knockers," Dutch said. "Plural. I think. The whole thing happened in the dark, of course. Did Tom say anything?"

"Nothing," Joe grunted. "He was concussed when he came to. Doc Lynch wouldn't let him talk. So how about you?"

"He's supposed to get home to bed," Janet protested sturdily. She moved over to stand beside Dutch. It made him feel protected and sympathized with. He liked it. But he said, "I'm all right, Jan. It'll only take a minute to tell."

He related succinctly the events leading up to the blow on his head. Everybody listened intently. Nobody interrupted him.

At the end of the recital Joe Barry said, "You got no idea at all of what these characters looked like?"

No.

"But you figure there were two of them?"

"Yes. A short kind of chunky one behind the flashlight, as near as I could tell. And the other one, the guy that hit me, was taller and thinner, I think, and kind of hunched over." Dutch laughed. "I thought for a second there it was a mummy attacking me!"

"What in heaven's name do you suppose they were after?" This was Dr. Kilty, looking around the Egyptian wing with a baffled expression on his face. "After all, very little of this stuff is original and valuable, you know," he explained to Sergeant Barry. "Most of our exhibits are merely fine replicas of the famous originals. You understand a modest museum like this one couldn't accumulate many original pieces."

Joe nodded his understanding.

"And besides," Dr. Kilty went on, warming to his subject, "now you couldn't possibly take original antiquities out of Egypt to display them in this museum or any other." He coughed. "It's against the law. All archaeological finds belong to the government." Kilty paused and looked guiltily at Dutch. "But I'm running on about nothing. What could the thieves have been after here, Dutch? Any ideas?"

"The petty cash in your office safe, maybe?"

Dr. Kilty shook his head. "Sergeant Barry and I took a look while Dr. Lynch was attending you and Tom. The office safe wasn't touched. There's no sign of anything else being touched, either."

"Except for a broken window in the basement," Barry amended, "where the men entered the museum. And that one exhibit case there beside you, Dutch."

Dutch noticed now that the plate-glass top of a nearby display case had been shattered.

"That could have been broken by you or Tom falling against it when you were attacked," Kilty suggested.

"Not Tom," Dutch said. "I'd have heard the glass break. All I heard was a thump." He looked at the broken display case again. "That's the case that holds some of our Tut-ankh-amen exhibits. Is anything missing from it?"

"I can't be sure. The things in the case are all mixed up—disarranged when the glass was smashed, I suppose. I didn't notice the gold fingernail covers when I checked hurriedly just now..." Dr. Kilty broke off. "But forget it for tonight, Dutch. Go home and get a good night's rest as Dr. Lynch advised. Take the day off tomorrow, too."

Dutch smiled. "With all this excitement going on? No, sir. Not a chance!"

"I'll talk to the night watchman tomorrow early," Barry said. "Maybe he saw something useful before he was hit."

Dutch stood up on wobbly legs. He felt very much in need of that good night's rest everybody kept advising him to get. Cam took him by one arm. Janet supported him tenderly on the other side. With Kathy trailing behind, they walked him to Cam's jalopy and helped him into the back seat.

"Pretty soft, old buddy," Cam said. "Two beautiful girls to help you in and out of cars and make a hero of you, just because you were dumb enough to get conked by a criminal! I should be so lucky!"

"Cam!" Janet began, furious with indignation. Then she saw by his wide grin that Cam was merely trying to ease Dutch's tension. She sat down quietly in the back seat beside Dutch.

Dutch was feeling a great deal better, now that he was out in the cool night air. "Kindly drive this hero home to bed," he said, "if you don't mind. What a night! I feel like a nickel's worth of nothing!"

The jalopy sputtered, purred, then headed for Dutch's house with a purposeful roar.

"Who could it possibly have been?" Janet asked several times during the brief ride.

Dutch said slowly as they pulled up before his house, "I don't know who. But something keeps nagging at me about the tall guy who lowered the boom on me."

"What do you mean 'nagging'?" Cam asked.

"Something about him seemed familiar."

"Familiar, he says." Cam grinned at the gills. "And he just admitted the whole thing happened in total darkness."

"Not quite," Dutch insisted. "I caught a quick look at this character in the reflected light from the flash, just before he used my head for a bongo drum. He was nothing but a dark blur, I'll admit. But something about that blur made me think I'd seen him before!"

* * * *

Quietly, so that he wouldn't disturb his mother and sister, both of whom were already asleep when he came in, Dutch undressed, climbed into his pajamas, and fell into bed, certain that he'd be asleep instantly.

It didn't work that way. Sleep refused to oblige him by shutting off his mental machinery until morning. He lay on his back, looking into darkness, trying to shed the obscure feeling that there had been something familiar about his tall attacker. The ache in his head, now gradually subsiding, was joined by crowding thoughts.

His adventure of the night played itself over and over for him like a tape recording. With each repetition of the tape he felt a growing conviction that he ought to be able to identify at least one of those shadowy figures he had encountered in the museum.

Despairing of sleep, he set himself to recalling as accurately as he could the events of recent weeks, raking his memory deliberately for anything that might be significant.

CHAPTER 3

Ancient History Pays Off

His official connection with the museum had started, he remembered, on the Friday of the week before school was to be over for the summer.

Mr. Jordan, who taught ancient history to juniors at Riverlawn High, asked Dutch to stay for a minute after class. When the other students had scattered noisily into the corridor, Mr. Jordan said to Dutch, "Have you any job lined up yet for the summer?"

"No, sir," Dutch said. "I've got applications in at the steel company and for lifeguard at Laurel Springs, but I haven't heard from either one yet. And it's late."

Mr. Jordan grinned a little. "Then you're still available?"

"Yes, sir." Dutch was puzzled. What kind of job could a teacher of ancient history offer him, he wondered.

"Do you know Dr. Kilty, Dutch? The curator of Fulmer Memorial Museum?"

Dutch shook his head. "No, sir. I know who he is, though." Dutch thought of the endless hours he'd spent prowling in Fulmer Museum when he should have been studying his algebra or English. "Why?"

"He's asked me to help him find a summer assistant. He wanted to know if I could recommend a good prospect. I recommended you."

Dutch was flabbergasted. "Thanks, Mr. Jordan," he said uncertainly. "But why me? What kind of job is it?"

"I recommended you because you are the best student in ancient history I've ever taught in this school, Dutch. You'll win the Fulmer Prize this year without any doubt. You have, I think, a genuine feeling for antiquity. It's a rare quality in a boy your age."

Mr. Jordan spread his hands in a disclaiming gesture. "I don't tell you this to flatter you, but to explain why I thought of you immediately for Dr. Kilty's job. The Fulmer Museum is strictly classical, you know that. It concerns itself exclusively with ancient Rome, Greece, and Egypt, because that's what the Fulmer Foundation limits it to. Mr. Fulmer was quite specific on that score when he endowed the museum for Riverlawn." Mr. Jordan smiled. "I guess he had a feeling for antiquity, too, as well as enough wealth to indulge it. Anyway, being interested in those ancient civilizations, and knowing something about them as you do, should make you more useful to Dr. Kilty this summer than anybody else I know."

Dutch felt a small pulse of excitement beginning to beat in his temple. "What's the job, then, Mr. Jordan?" he asked. "Has it actually something to do with the exhibits themselves?"

"Dr. Kilty told me he wants somebody who can help him re-label, re-catalogue, and rearrange the Egyptian exhibits."

"Boy!" breathed Dutch.

"Are you interested?"

"I certainly am, Mr. Jordan!"

"Good. I was sure you would be. Get over to the museum and tell Dr. Kilty I sent you. He'll interview you."

"When?"

"This afternoon. As soon as you've finished your last class."

"How about track practice?"

"Skip it. This is far more important."

"Okay," Dutch said. "And Mr. Jordan. Thanks a million for giving me a chance at this."

"Forget it. I just hope you'll be able to nail down the job, Dutch. Good luck."

* * * *

After school Dutch found Cam Osborn in the locker room preparing to change into track clothes for the afternoon's practice. Cam put the shot and threw the discus on the Riverlawn High team. Being big, muscular, and well-coordinated, he brought to these field events the same outstanding performance he exhibited as an all-state halfback on the Riverlawn football team. He was Dutch's best friend.

His stalwart frame, calm mien, blue eyes, and blondness were in striking contrast to Dutch's slightness, intense face, short-cut black hair, and dark eyes. The two boys had entered Riverlawn High together but from different elementary schools. They happened to be assigned swimming lockers next to each other, and their friendship began when they swam a dead heat in a fifty-yard race informally arranged on the first day of swimming classes. This friendship, through constant association in classes and on athletic teams, had grown stronger each term since. Now, at the end of their junior year, the boys were inseparable companions.

"Listen, Cam," Dutch said, slightly breathless. "I'm going to skip practice today."

"My, my!" Cam grinned at him. "The Flying Dutchman of Riverlawn High himself! Don't you need practice to win that mile tomorrow, son?"

"I'll run just as fast against Dowingdale tomorrow as if I'd practiced all day today," Dutch returned. "I'm going job hunting."

"Job hunting? Where?"

With a straight face Dutch said, "The Fulmer Memorial Museum."

Cam pretended shock. "You're kidding! What's the job? Cutting grass and trimming hedges? What else could you do around a museum, Dutch? Oh, I know. Wash windows."

"You forget, no doubt, that I am an intellectual, an egghead. An expert in ancient history, that's what your short friend is, friend. Ask Mr. Jordan. I'm in a hurry, Cam, no fooling. Come down to Cox's tonight and I'll tell you how my interview went. Okay?"

Sure.

"Only thing I'm afraid is that the job might not pay enough," said Dutch. "I've got to get a pretty decent deal. And with a museum…"

"The Fulmer Foundation is loaded. Everybody knows that. They'll pay plenty if you're working for them. Would you be?"

"Yeah. As an assistant to the curator."

"Wow! That sounds a lot better than the road-gang job my dad's getting me through one of his clients."

"The pay's probably peanuts."

"How do you know? Go see the man and find out. Maybe they pay a thousand bucks a month. Take off, will you? I'll see you tonight at Cox's. And I'll even tell the coach why you're not at practice."

"Thanks." Dutch hurried off.

"Good luck," Cam called after him.

Dutch could tell from the deliberately bantering tone of Cam's voice that his friend was trying to hide his earnest hope that Dutch would get a lucrative summer job. For Cam knew as well as Dutch how much he needed one.

Several years before, after a trip abroad to buy cotton for the textile firm that employed him, Dutch's father had died suddenly from something he'd picked up in his travels—hepatitis, Dr. Lynch had said. Dutch's mother, a frail, frequently ailing, but high-spirited woman, was left with Dutch and his sister Hilda to raise and educate, but without very much money to do it with. Mrs. Schildecker had obtained a job as bookkeeper at Beeson's Department Store and had managed to keep a roof over her children's heads and enough food on the table. It would have been impossible to make ends meet, however, without the extra money that Dutch brought in from his evening job as counterman at Cox's Dairy Store and his earnings from the full-time jobs he had managed to get each summer since his father's death. Even Hilda, who was only fourteen, contributed to the family finances by frequent baby-sitting assignments from Riverlawn families.

Leaving the school grounds, Dutch thought briefly of Cam's circumstances, so different from his own. For Campbell Baxter Osborn III was an only child. His father was one of Riverlawn's most successful attorneys. Cam's mother was a stately woman whose cool blond looks and warm disposition had been passed on to Cam. The Osborns lived in a large fashionable house. They had several servants. They had two cars in addition to Cam's jalopy. And they had a soaring pride in their only son.

Yet Dutch knew that Cam was neither spoiled by the affluence of his parents nor conceited about his own good looks and athletic prowess. At seventeen he took all this for granted and enjoyed himself thoroughly.

Dutch felt very lucky to have him for a friend.

Dr. Kilty, the curator of Fulmer Memorial Museum, was a stooped, scholarly-looking man of under medium height, with a benign, almost cherubic, smile that twisted his sandy mustache askew in a curiously appealing way. He wore steel-framed glasses, rusty black slacks, and a flowing bow tie. But to these sober items of apparel Dr. Kilty added a sports jacket of such a violent scarlet-black-and-blue plaid that he was clearly visible, like a neon sign, five blocks away.

Looking quizzically across his desk at his young visitor, he asked Dutch only four questions. The first one caught Dutch off guard.

"What were your midterm grades, Schildecker?"

"In ancient history?" Dutch asked.

"No. Mr. Jordan told me that one. Your other subjects."

Dutch flushed. "I'm afraid they weren't very good, sir. I just get by, usually." He told Dr. Kilty his grades.

"Definitely and decidedly average," Dr. Kilty said. "One can't call them more." His lips curved and his mustache tilted. "Means nothing, however. Not when you get ninety-seven in ancient history. Merely means you aren't very interested in the other subjects, right?" His speech was energetic, staccato. It seemed more in keeping with his loud sports jacket than with his scholarly position.

Dutch gulped. "I hadn't thought of it that way, but perhaps you're right, sir. I hope so."

"Second question," said Dr. Kilty abruptly, "and I want an absolutely Honest answer to this one, Schildecker. It won't prejudice your chances of getting the job, whatever you say. But answer honestly. Agreed?"

"Sure," Dutch said, wondering what was coming.

"All right. Suppose, then, you're a rich man's son. You've got no financial problems. You don't need to take a job at all this summer. You hear about this job being open. Would you be likely to apply for it anyway?"

"Yes, sir," said Dutch promptly.

"Work with me here all summer long for *nothing*, just for the chance to expand your knowledge of the ancient civilizations we're concerned with?"

"Yes, sir." Dutch answered again without hesitation and with emphasis.

"Good." The curator's crooked smile came again. "I believe you would at that. Now then. Look at this card. It's one of our label cards from an exhibit, as you can see. From our Egyptian section."

Dutch read the brief inscription on the printed card. It said merely:

REPRODUCTION OF THE ROYAL
CARTOUCHE OF THOTMES III

"Now this one," Dr. Kilty said. He handed Dutch another card. It said:

REPRODUCTION OF A WALL DECORATION AT
DEIR EL BAHARI, SHOWING KING TUTHMOSIS
III IN THE PRESENCE OF THE GOD ANUBIS

"Any comment?" Dr. Kilty asked.

Dutch swallowed hard. "Without seeing the exhibits, sir, I can't very well comment…"

The curator said, "No, no. What I mean is, which one of those cards spells the name of the Pharaoh correctly?"

"Oh," Dutch said with relief. "They're both okay, I think, sir. Aren't there any number of acceptable ways to spell the name Thotmes? I think it can be Thotmes, Thothmes, Thutmos, Thutmase, Thutmose, Thutmoses, or Thutmosis, to name a few."

Dr. Kilty sat back in his chair. "How's that happen?"

"Well, I've read that nobody's absolutely certain of the exact transliteration of the ancient Egyptian hieroglyphs into English, sir. With their hieratic and demotic variations, and the confusion of the Greek, Coptic, and Arabic languages that came into Egypt later…"

"Well, well," Dr. Kilty interrupted him. His eyes shone behind his steel-rimmed glasses. "Mr. Jordan has taught you something, hasn't he? You're right about King Tothmes' name. It can be spelled a lot of ways. And unfortunately it is spelled differently on almost every card in our museum that refers to him. As new exhibits have been added over the years, each curator has apparently used his own favored spelling of the name on exhibit labels and in our catalog file. You can see how confusing this is for museum visitors and my staff?"

Dutch nodded but said nothing.

"And that's only one of hundreds of examples of confused data. I want to clear up some of this confusion this summer, Schildecker. I intend to do a lot of relabeling, re-cataloguing, rearranging of our

Egyptian exhibits." He slapped his desk. "My staff has its regular duties to perform, of course. They can't help me very much with this extracurricular job, since vacations interfere and summer is our busiest season. So I'd like you to help me, as a special summer assistant."

With a sense of exhilaration Dutch thought, I'm in. He likes me. I can have this job if I want it. And I do want it. I want it badly. But does it pay enough?

He opened his mouth to ask, feeling hopeful and hopeless at the same time. But Dr. Kilty gave him no chance for speech; he swept smoothly on, waving a hand for silence.

"Which brings me to my final question in this interview," he said briskly. "How much money did you make in whatever job you had last summer? And how much were you expecting—or shall I say, hoping—to make this summer?" Dr. Kilty's mustache drew a very crooked line across his face as he smiled broadly. "I may tell you, before you answer, young man, that I am empowered by the trustees of the Fulmer Foundation to pay you an amount for this summer's work equal to whichever of those two figures is the greater, as the income tax people express it." He paused briefly.

Dutch supplied a figure. Then Dr. Kilty asked, "What do you say, Schildecker?"

Dutch had been too excited and grateful to do anything but nod his head and mumble his thanks.

* * * *

When he had reached home that day, he'd gone into the small living room, tossed his jacket on the sofa, and yelled "Mom!"

No answer. Still at work, he thought worriedly. They're working her overtime again. "Hilda!" he called then.

His sister came through the swinging door between dining room and kitchen. "I'm here, Oscar," she said sweetly, knowing the use of his given name infuriated her brother. "Second choice, obviously, since you called Mother first, but what do you want?"

"To see if anybody's home, that's all," Dutch said. "Don't be so sensitive. And don't call me Oscar."

"It's your name."

"So it's my name. But that doesn't mean I like it. You call me Dutch, Hilda, or…"

"Or what?"

Hilda stood in the kitchen doorway, her hands wet from the water in which she had been washing the vegetables for dinner. She started the dinner every day to save her mother from having to do the whole job when she returned from work. Hilda was already as tall as her mother and only three inches shorter than Dutch. She was blessed with a creamy complexion, golden-red hair, and wide, innocent-seeming eyes that masked the mischievous, alert mind behind them.

He grinned at her. "Or nothing. You're a good kid, Hilda."

"Well," she replied. "From you, that's something."

"Wait. You didn't let me finish. You're a good kid except for two things."

She sniffed.

"For one thing, you're a girl," Dutch went on in a teasing tone. "That's bad in itself. For another, you're a boy-crazy girl. And that's the worst kind."

Hilda said with dignity, "I intend to be a wife and mother some day. That's my chosen goal in life, smarty. And I don't see anything wrong with starting to like the boys now—while I'm still young."

"Some wife and mother you'll make!" Dutch laughed. "Got a condition in domestic science!"

She tossed her head and turned back to the kitchen. "Listen to who's talking! *You* almost failed every subject except ancient history, and only a nut would like that dry old stuff!"

Dutch said seriously, "It's not dry at all, Hilda." He walked to the kitchen door and said to her back, "And besides, sister, I have a very superior brain, whether you know it or not."

She ignored that as not worthy of notice. "Did you see Cam Osborn today?"

"Of course I saw him."

"Oh, you lucky man!" Hilda scraped a carrot in the sink. "He's absolutely the most wonderfully dreamy boy in the whole school!"

"Hey! Lay off that stuff! It's sickening!" Dutch said. "For Pete's sake, Hilda, Cam's a grown man and you're still a baby. A freshman! And Cam likes Kathy Johnson, anyway. You know that."

She acted as though she hadn't heard him. "Cam Osborn," she whispered dramatically. "Yum!"

Dutch left her in disgust. What a girl!

* * * *

The chief topic of conversation at dinner that night had been Dutch's summer job in the museum. Mrs. Schildecker was as pleased as Dutch was about it.

"It'll be a wonderful summer for you, Dutch," she said happily. "I'm so glad for you."

"And the pay is great," Dutch said. "I'll earn more than I did last summer with the tree nursery." He smiled at his mother. "And when we add that to your salary at Beeson's…"

"And my baby-sitting fortune," Hilda chimed in. "…we'll be in pretty fair shape for next year."

Dutch paused. "And that'll be my last year of high school. After that, naturally, I can *really* help out, Mom."

His mother smiled at him and sighed. "I wish there were some way we could afford to send you to college, Dutch. That's what your father would have wanted for you more than anything in the world."

"We've been all over that, Mom. It's out. I'd like to go to college, of course. Who wouldn't? But I'm a pretty poor student, after all. Except in ancient history," he added quickly before Hilda could do it. "So I can't get a scholarship anywhere on my high school record."

"If you were Cam Osborn now," the irrepressible Hilda said, "you could get a football scholarship someplace."

"I sure could," Dutch said. "Cam's been secretly offered two or three propositions already and he's not even a senior yet!" He shook his head. "But he's a great football player, really great. And I'm just a mediocre miler, I'm afraid." There was no self-pity or bitterness in his tone, but Dutch's mother reached out and patted his hand.

"You could earn your way through college," she said quietly. "Lots of boys do. Hilda and I could get along all right without your help for four years, I'm sure. Couldn't we, Hilda?"

"Certainly," said Hilda with great disdain. "Who needs him?"

Dutch laughed. "Well, that was a good try. But you know darn well that if I don't get a steady job as soon as I finish high school,

Hilda never will finish and you'll ruin your health, Mom, working so hard. The doctor told you to slow down, remember?"

Struck by a new idea, Hilda said, "Listen, Dutch. If I married a fairly rich boy, I could get him to pay your way through college and take care of Mom, too. After all, as my husband, he'd have some responsibility for my relatives, wouldn't he?"

Dutch hooted. "How about that, Mom? She's fourteen years old and she's going to marry a millionaire to send me through college! The child bride! That'll be the day, Hilda. You're sick, kid."

"In a mere six years I'll be twenty," Hilda replied with spirit. "And it seems to me, Oscar, that twenty is plenty old enough…"

"Children!" Mrs. Schildecker laughed and held out a hand to quiet them.

"Well," said Dutch, "let's get the dishes done, huh? I'm due at Cox's for work at seven. Cam's coming down."

"Give him my love," Hilda said sweetly. "I think he's a darling boy, Mom, don't you?" Then, inconsequentially, "Did I tell you that a secondhand man was here today?"

"Secondhand man?"

"The best-looking thing! He was looking for secondhand things to buy. He had a straight, beautiful nose, and black eyebrows that stuck out like bushes, and a darling black mustache. Very distinguished-looking, I thought. And quite short—about like me."

"You didn't let him in? When you were here alone?" Mrs. Schildecker was disturbed.

"No. Anyway, I wasn't actually here yet. He was standing on the porch when I came home from Rita's. And he asked if we had any old luggage or silver or things he could buy. I told him no. And he finally went away." Hilda rolled her eyes. "He was the cutest little man!"

"She's man-crazy," Dutch said with a frown at his sister. He got up from the table. "See if you can't talk some sense into her, Mom, okay?"

He began to carry dishes out to the kitchen.

CHAPTER 4

The Man on the Ladder

The next day Dutch had broken the school record for the mile. He won the event from a tall lanky runner named Lister in River-lawn's home meet with Dowingdale High School. His time was the best of his career: 4:32.

"Not bad for a short-legged little midget like you!" Cam beamed at him after the race while Dutch was getting his breath. "Now you've got a new mile record and a cushy summer job, too."

"I feel good," Dutch admitted.

"Me, too. Strong as a horse. I think I'll throw the discus over the schoolhouse today, just for the fun of it. And get a school record for myself to go with yours."

"You can do it easy. Listen, Cam. Since they called the mile run early today, I can get in an hour's rest before dinner if I leave here now. I'm pretty tired, and I've got to work at Cox's tonight. Coach said it was okay to leave. So I'm going home. I'll see you later, right?"

"Right. I'll drop into Cox's."

"With two gold medals, I hope."

"Call me Muscles." Cam smiled. "I can't miss."

Dutch said, "Oh, and clean out our locker when you dress, will you? This is the last meet, so we're supposed to take our track stuff home."

"Okay. But leave our traveling bag for me to tote the stuff in, huh?"

"Yeah." Cam was referring to the worn leather suitcase which belonged to Dutch and which they used jointly to carry their equipment on athletic trips away from Riverlawn. "We won't be needing it again till fall. Keep it at your house if you like."

"That's a pretty sneaky way to get me to wash out your dirty old track uniforms, Buster!"

Dutch grinned.

"But all right," Cam said. "Go home and rest, Champ. See you later."

* * * *

The walk home from the school served to cool Dutch off gradually and keep his muscles from stiffening up. When he dropped onto the bed in his room, he was more than ready for a nap. He had the house to himself. Hilda and her friend Rita had been spectators at the track meet, he knew, and would stay until the last event was run off. And his mother was still at work. Drowsily he thought how lucky he'd been to beat Lister and make a new school record, and how nice it was to be able to get home for a nap an hour early. He relaxed and fell asleep at once.

Half an hour later something awakened him. Groggily he opened his eyes. He lay quiet, listening. He became conscious of a scraping sound that seemed to come from the side of the house, outside the window of his bedroom.

Dutch got off the bed and went to the window which he had left half raised before lying down. He looked out.

On the ground below, a tall man was carefully placing an extension ladder against the side of the house, its upper end scraping against the wooden outer wall of the attic above Dutch's room.

Dutch looked more closely at the man at the foot of the ladder. He was dressed in new blue jeans and an open-necked shirt. On his head he wore a golf cap with a big bill. While Dutch watched, the man lifted the golf cap to wipe his perspiring forehead, and Dutch saw that he was partially bald, clean-shaven, brown-haired. He wore black sunglasses. And he was a perfect stranger.

Dutch thought to himself, now what? Can't a guy even get a little sleep on a Saturday afternoon without a house painter leaning ladders against the house? But he would have known if his mother had arranged to have any painting done. So who was this character?

Moved by a wayward impulse to mischief, Dutch drew back from the window and waited until the vibration of the ladder-end against the house wall told him that the man had begun to mount.

Even then he hesitated for another moment or two until he thought the man had climbed high enough to be about on a level with his second floor window. Then he suddenly stuck his head out of the window, swiveled it toward the stranger, and said, "Hi!"

The man nearly fell off the ladder. He made a wild grab at the sidebars, steadied himself, and then clung there as though he had been frozen in place, with one foot lifted to reach for the next rung. He took a deep breath and hunched his thin shoulders up around his neck, almost like a man waiting to be struck by a whip. Only when he had exhaled deliberately did he slowly turn his head to stare through his sunglasses at Dutch's face, scarcely ten feet from his own.

Dutch couldn't see his eyes behind the dark lenses. A hard, thin-lipped mouth made a straight gash across the broad face. With a visible effort the man summoned a grin.

"You scared me, kid," he said in a hoarse voice.

"I'm sorry," said Dutch, already feeling guilty, "but you scared me, too. Your ladder woke me up."

The man slowly put his foot—the airborne one—down on the ladder rung. "I didn't think there was anyone home," he said then, with a trace of sharpness.

"There isn't, except me. Who are you?"

"Television repair. Got a call to look over your aerial lead-in."

"There's nothing wrong with our television. At least it was okay last night. Who called you?"

The man shrugged. "All I know, bud, the boss says come and look at your roof aerial. Whoever called in says your lead-in wire is broken at the chimney. I'm just going up to the roof." The man's words came out fluently enough, but something about their inflection gave Dutch the impression that he was not completely sure of himself in his use of idiomatic American. He stood very still on the ladder. "I rang your doorbell but nobody answered," he said with an injured air.

Dutch had a feeling this was the truth. Maybe it was the doorbell which had first disturbed his nap. "I was asleep," he apologized, sorry now that he had startled this harmless repairman who was obviously just trying to do his job. "Are you new in Riverlawn? I don't think I've seen you around."

"This is my first week. And what a business! Half your life you spend on a ladder! Oh, well. I'll go on up and look at your wire if you don't mind. I got other calls to make today."

Automatically Dutch tilted his head back and looked upward toward the top of the house, trying to see the TV aerial on the roof, but it was hidden by the overhanging eaves. "There's no use going up, Mister," he said positively. "I know our lead-in's okay. You must have a wrong address."

The man fumbled in his shirt pocket, brought out a scrap of paper and consulted it. "Isn't this Seventh Street? One-o-four Seventh? Connors' house?"

"This is one-o-four Seventeenth Street," Dutch said. "And our name isn't Connors. It's Schildecker. You're about ten blocks out. I'm sorry."

"Seventeenth!" the man muttered in disgust. He thrust the scrap of paper angrily back into his pocket, but it escaped his fingers and dropped to the ground unnoticed. He started to descend the ladder. "Sorry I bothered you, bud." He reached the ground, dropped the upper section of his extension ladder down on its ratchet and wearily hung the heavy ladder over one shoulder.

As he disappeared around the corner of the house Dutch belatedly called, "Hey! You dropped your paper!" The man ignored him, or didn't hear him.

Dutch went back to bed and resumed his interrupted nap.

* * * *

That night, Dutch had recounted the incident to Cam.

Cam was perched on a high stool in front of the milk bar of Cox's Daily Store, sipping a milkshake through a straw and basking comfortably in the remembered pleasure of winning two first-place medals at the track meet that afternoon.

"This TV repairman nearly did a nose dive off his ladder when I poked my head out," Dutch said with gusto. "Boy, was he ever surprised! Then I started to be sorry I'd scared him when I found out he had the wrong address."

"Served him right," Cam said lazily, "for waking up a weary athlete. Where was he from?"

Dutch shrugged. "Just a TV repairman."

"From where? What company'd he work for? They ought to be told they've got a repairman who doesn't know his way around town and wakes up the wrong people."

Dutch thought for a second. "He didn't say what company he worked for. He was a new man on the job, anyway."

"What'd his truck say on it?"

"I couldn't see his truck from my back window."

"Oh, well." Cam yawned. "What's the difference?" He emptied his milkshake carton with a sucking sound, leaned back on his stool, and stretched. "School's almost over for another year, Dutch," he said with satisfaction. He looked across the counter at his friend, who was dipping rainbow ice cream for a cone almost as big as the little boy who had ordered it.

To Cam's surprise Dutch was frowning; his face wore a serious, preoccupied expression. Cam said lightly, "Don't frown at the ice cream, friend. It's bad advertising. What's wrong? Does it make you cranky to win a mile race and set a school record?"

Dutch laughed then. But he said slowly, "No, I feel okay. It's just that…" He paused.

"It's just that what?"

"I just remembered a funny thing about that ladder this afternoon."

"I'm laughing already. What?"

"You know when I stopped the TV man as he was going up onto the roof?"

Cam nodded.

"Well, I looked up toward the roof, too, kind of automatically."

"So?"

"It seems to me now that there was something strange about the ladder. It was in two sections. And it was extended as far as it would go."

"What's so funny about that?"

Dutch said thoughtfully, "It wasn't nearly long enough to reach the roof. It only went up as far as our attic window."

Cam stared at him, uncomprehending for a moment. "Are you cracking up, buddy?"

"That ladder was at least six feet too short to reach the roof."

"But he said he was going up to the roof?"

"He sure did."

Cam ran a muscular hand through his short hair. "That's kind of funny, all right," he said. Then he shook his head. "You must be wrong about the ladder, Dutch. Maybe he didn't have the third section extended yet. He meant to do it when he got higher up."

"There wasn't any third section." Dutch was stubborn. "He couldn't have gone any higher than the attic window. In fact, now I think of it, the upper end of the ladder was resting on the sill of our attic window."

"Maybe the guy was a psycho," Cam suggested weakly. "A nut that goes around climbing the side of people's houses."

"He didn't talk like a nut. He talked pretty good English, too, come to think of it. Almost as though he was trying to use American slang right but couldn't quite make the grade. Know what I mean?"

"So don't get in an uproar. After all, the man rang your doorbell. If he was a phony, he wouldn't have done that."

"He *said* he rang the doorbell. But I didn't hear it. I was asleep. And besides, he could have rung it to make sure nobody was home, maybe."

Cam tapped his temple with a big forefinger. "Let's figure this out logically, Sherlock," he said. "I'll put my brilliant wits to work. Meanwhile, please give me a big rainbow ice cream cone like the one you just built for that little kid. It will help me think."

Dutch reached for the dipper with a laugh. "The big spender. You'll make Cox's day. One jumbo rainbow coming up." He passed the cone to Cam and dropped Cam's dime into the cash register with a clatter. "Now, what's the solution, big brain?" he asked as Cam rotated the cone on his tongue with relish.

Cam tapped his temple again. "I've got it, Watson," he said seriously. "This TV character of yours must have thought nobody was home, that your house was empty. He rang the doorbell to make sure, just as you say. And when nobody answered the bell, he figured he could go right ahead and rob you blind in broad daylight, since he was disguised as a TV repairman. He was heading for that attic window, that's what I think."

Dutch said, "You may have a point. None of us was supposed to be home, anyway. Mother at work, Hilda and I at the track meet. It was purest chance that I finished my race early today and came home for a rest. But that assumes the guy knew we'd all be out of the house—that he knows our habits and everything."

"Maybe he's got brilliant wits, too, like me."

"If he has, he wouldn't pick out our house to rob, for Pete's sake! Nothing in the place's worth a nickel at a pawnshop."

"So we're wrong. He was legitimate. And he just happened to bring too short a ladder. Happens every day. Especially to guys who are new on the roof-climbing circuit. And he was. You said so."

"He said so. But I guess you're right. Like a plumber bringing the wrong wrench to the job, you mean?"

Cam nodded. Then he suddenly said, "Hey! Am I sharp to-night? I got another idea."

"What?"

"We can settle this thing easy, one way or the other."

"Plow?"

"Simple. Bring me the telephone book from your booth back there, my good man."

Puzzled, Dutch complied.

"Now," said Cam, smiling complacently, "I believe you told me that your TV man had the wrong address?"

"Yeah."

"And he said he was supposed to be on Seventh Street?"

Dutch got it now. He felt excitement. "Right. And he asked if our name wasn't Connors. So if we find somebody named Connors listed in the phone book who lives at 104 Seventh Street…"

"Sure." Cam started to leaf through the telephone book to the C's.

He found four Connors listed.

But none of them lived anywhere near Seventh Street.

"Whee!" breathed Cam softly. "Maybe the guy *was* a crook, after all."

Just then Dutch happened to glance toward the front of the store where another counterman was selling delicatessen items. For an instant Dutch's eyes rested on the big display window there, liberally plastered with advertising streamers. And flashingly, be-tween two of the paper signs, he was aware of a man peering in the show window. When Dutch's glance reached the watcher's face, it withdrew immediately from sight with what seemed to Dutch an almost guilty haste.

He said to Cam, "I think somebody was watching me through the front window just now."

Cam turned swiftly on his stool. "Nobody there now."

"He took off when I noticed him."

"Who was it?"

"Never saw him before," said Dutch.

"What'd he look like?"

"Big face with fat cheeks was all I got a glimpse of."

"Fatty Duveen," said Cam comfortably. "He gets his kicks looking in Cox's windows since the doc put him on a diet."

"It wasn't Fatty." Dutch frowned. "There was something familiar about him, though." Dutch suddenly snapped his fingers. "His shoulders were kind of hunched up around his neck. Like that TV man's this afternoon."

"Take it easy, pal," Cam said. "You're dreaming up a storm."

"In a pig's eye!" Dutch said. "I saw somebody. Hey, Smitty!" he called to the front counterman. "Take a squint through the window and see if anybody's hanging around outside, will you?"

Smitty looked out, then called back agreeably, "Nobody, Dutch. A big guy across the street in Siminds' doorway, smoking. Who were you expecting? Cleopatra?"

"Thanks," Dutch said. He turned to Cam. "It's almost closing time. Will you do me a favor? Go out our back way into the alley, go around the building, and keep an eye on that big guy across the street until I get off duty, huh? It *could* be that it's the TV man who was up to something funny at home today. If it is, I'd sure like to know. And if he's watching me, he'll hang around out there."

Cam said good-naturedly, "The boy detective. Well, it just happens you've picked yourself the finest eye in the business, Chester. Show me the back door and I'll be glad to make like Ellery Queen. First chance I ever had to shadow anybody. I'll have a ball."

He slipped off his stool and ambled casually toward Cox's back door. "See you, Dutch," he said over his shoulder. Then he was gone.

Twenty minutes later, when Dutch had cleaned up for the night and collected his weekly pay from Mr. Cox, he, too, left the store by the back way.

Keeping a sharp lookout, he slowly negotiated the dark alley behind the store and made the turn around the building corner toward Main Street on which Cox's faced. There, lurking in shadow, he found Cam.

Dutch came up quietly behind him and said, "Boo!" Cam jumped. "Don't do that, Buster," he muttered out of the side of his mouth, tough-guy style. "You want to spoil my aim?"

"Who are you aiming at? My TV man?"

"I doubt it. The big guy you sent me to watch is currently sitting over there in Parrish's Bar having a quiet beer."

"Must be an innocent citizen, then. Thanks for the private-eye act. Let's hit for home."

"Wait!" Cam hissed. "Here comes the subject now." He pretended to write in an imaginary notebook. "Subject left Parrish's saloon at ten thirty-three."

Sure enough, a large figure had come out of Parrish's and was walking away from them up Main Street, too far away for Dutch to get a good look at him. He could see that it was a tallish man, slightly stooped or hunched, but that was all.

"Come on!" Cam whispered, caught up in his enthusiasm for playing private eye. "Let's trail him."

They waited until the big man was two blocks away. Then they cautiously emerged into Main Street and followed him at a sedate pace, trying to look inconspicuous as they walked under the corner street light and past the neon-illuminated fronts of Riverlawn's business district.

After several blocks, they saw the man turn off Main Street toward South Side. They nudged each other, then ran along the grass fringe of the sidewalk for a hundred paces to close the gap between them and their quarry. They didn't want to lose him at the turn-off.

They needn't have worried. When they rounded the corner carefully, the man was plainly visible ahead of them, stepping along at a casual pace, obviously unaware he was being followed. He was whistling when he arrived at Jefferson Square. This was a square of shabby, run-down houses, once the homes of prominent Riverlawn citizens at the turn of the century, but now converted into inexpensive boarding houses, second-rate bars, and third-rate hotels.

Dutch said, "You hear that funny tune he's whistling?"

"Yeah. Kind of a hootchy-kootchy number."

"As a famous private eye, does that mean to you that he's Persian or Turkish or Arabic or something like that?"

"Naw," said Cam impatiently. "This guy has just had a couple of beers and is feeling like some kootch music, that's all. Look, he's going into that trap on the corner."

They halted and watched the tall figure mount the steps of a former mansion now badly in need of paint. There was a neon sign over the porch roof that read "Doheny's Hotel." As the man passed under the sign and pulled open the hotel's double glass doors, they got a good look at him at last.

He was tall, all right. Just about the size of the TV man, Dutch decided. And like the TV man, he had thin shoulders that he carried slightly hunched up around his neck. He was wearing a suit and a jaunty checked hat with a narrow brim. His face, in the light of the open door was broad, but the lips were thick, the cheeks rounded and fuller than those of the TV repairman had been. As he went into the hotel, he removed his gay hat and carried it in his hand.

Dutch said to Cam, "That's it. We don't need to go any farther."

"How come? Isn't he your TV man?"

"Not a chance."

"How can you tell from this distance?"

"He's fatter in the face, fuller in the lips. And did you see him take off his hat?"

"Sure."

"He has a full head of black hair. The TV man had brown hair and was half bald."

"Too bad," Cam said. "I was just beginning to get a charge out of this detective work."

"Even Ellery Queen makes mistakes sometimes. And I guess I made two of them today. First, I suspected an innocent TV man of sinister doings."

"Innocent? How about that phony address for Connors' house?" Cam was reluctant to give up his theory about that.

"He probably copied it down wrong, being new at it. And brought the wrong ladder for the same reason."

"Could be, I guess."

"Yeah. And my second mistake was trailing this bird home from his Saturday night out at Parrish's."

"It was fun," Cam said. "A red herring, isn't that what they call it?"

"Let's go home, Cam, what do you say?"

"Roger."

* * * *

By his luminous wrist watch dial, Dutch saw that it was two o'clock in the morning. He was as far from sleep as ever. The ache in his head, all that now remained to remind him that he had been knocked unconscious tonight at the museum, was gradually subsiding.

But he thought he finally had put his finger on it—the thing in these recalled events that might account for the odd feeling that he had seen his shadowy attacker before.

It comes down to this, he decided: I've got a thing about hunched shoulders, that's all. When I tried to describe the man who slugged me tonight, I told Joe Barry he was tall and kind of hunched. That TV man on the ladder outside my room had hunched shoulders, too, and he was tall. So I must be making a connection between the two guys just because they're both tall and carry their shoulders high. That's all I was going on when Cam and I trailed the beer drinker home that night. Hunched shoulders. But he turned out to be an entirely different guy from the TV man. So what about this hunched shoulders impression? It's probably screwy. But maybe I'd better tell Joe Barry about the TV man tomorrow, anyway, just for laughs.

Not that there's much chance this business at the museum tonight had anything to do with me personally at all. It was just a couple of burglars who were interrupted in the middle of a job, by Tom first and then by me. But if so, what in heck were they after in the museum? Certainly not just those fake fingernail covers in the Tut-ankh-amen display case. If, that is, the fingernail covers were actually stolen, anyway. They may be there in the morning when we check...

At this point tired muscles, weary brain, aching head, and general frustration took over, and Dutch fell asleep like a stone dropping into a pool of water.

CHAPTER 5

The False Fingertips

In the morning Dutch woke up feeling as fit as though his skull and a blunt instrument could not possibly have come together violently less than twelve hours ago.

He was rested, hungry, and anxious to get to the museum as soon as possible.

He told his mother and Hilda at breakfast what had happened to him the night before, belittling the blow on his head to reassure his mother.

"Just a tap," he told them, indicating the spot below his ear. "See, the lump has gone down. And it isn't even sore this morning."

"But Dutch!" his mother protested, "you might have been hurt quite badly!" She was shocked. "I don't want you working in that place at night—or even in the daytime—if things like that can happen there!"

For ten minutes, then, Dutch talked rapidly and persuasively, denying further danger, trying to calm his mother's anxiety, making light of his experience. He didn't want his mother to worry, of course. And especially he didn't want her to insist that he give up his job at the museum.

Hilda helped him. She thought the whole thing thrilling. "Too bad Cam didn't come for you a little sooner," she said rather unsympathetically, "because if he'd run into those burglars, I bet he'd have knocked *them* out!"

Dutch laughed. "Your hero. Well, he might, at that." He got up from the breakfast table. "I've got to rush, Mom. Don't worry about me, will you? I'll see you at dinner. Good-by. 'By, Hilda."

"You tell that policeman friend of yours…" his mother began.

"Joe Barry?"

"Yes. You tell him I think it's disgraceful that the Riverlawn Police Department allows such things to happen in a public museum!"

"I'll tell him," Dutch promised. "But I don't know how much good it will do."

* * * *

As he entered the Egyptian Hall of the museum a few minutes later Dutch's eyes went immediately to the broken exhibit case near the center of the room. He walked up the marble aisle toward it, thinking how friendly and unmenacing this vaulted well-lighted hall seemed this morning, compared with the sinister, almost evil aura it had worn last night while bathed in darkness and spawning violence.

A man from the museum's maintenance crew was measuring the top frame of the broken display case. Dutch knew he was preparing to install a new sheet of glass in the case, replacing the one shattered last night.

Dutch greeted him; then he stood and looked down for a moment into the case. It had originally contained replicas of a few of the smaller articles recovered from Tut-ankh-amen's tomb: a heavy gold bracelet decorated with a large lapis-lazuli scarab; a statuette in gold of King Tut-ankh-amen, crowned with the red crown of lower Egypt, standing upon a flat boat in the act of casting a harpoon; an alabaster model boat with carved ibex heads for prow and stern; three Shawabti, or funerary statuettes, made of brownish wood, their arms crossed at the breast; several gold necklaces; two gold finger rings; some graceful cosmetic jars; and five golden fingernail covers set with semiprecious stones. The exhibits in the case had already been returned to their velvet-lined places, Dutch saw. All except the Pharaoh's fingertips.

They were gone.

Dr. Kilty had left word for Dutch to come into his office as soon as he arrived. When Dutch entered, Kilty waved him to a chair and began without preliminary, his staccato speech more emphatic than ever. "You all right, Dutch?"

"Fine."

"Good. Sergeant Barry has already talked with Tom this morning. Tom's fine, too. Going to stay quiet for another day, though. Dr. Lynch's orders."

"Gee, I'm glad they didn't hurt Tom seriously," Dutch said with relief. "What did he have to say?"

"Very little. He didn't see as much as you did. He was making his rounds as usual, checking one wing after the other. He came out of the Roman wing into the lobby a few minutes before ten. He looked through the archway into Egyptian Hall. It was totally dark. His night light wasn't burning. He thought the bulb had burned out."

"Had it?" asked Dutch.

"No. Just been unscrewed in the socket."

"Oh."

"Deliberately unscrewed, obviously, to lure Tom into the room. Tom walked into the trap. As he approached the night light with his flashlight on, something came out of the dark and hit him. Just as it hit you. That's all he knows."

"Where, sir?" asked Dutch.

"Left side of the head."

"I mean where in the Egyptian wing? Near the broken display case?"

"As far as he can remember, Tom wasn't near enough to fall against it or break it when he went down."

"Then the burglars broke it for sure?"

"No question about it," Dr. Kilty said grimly. "I've checked against our master inventory list this morning. Everything's still there. Except Tut-ankh-amen's fingertips."

"All five of them," Dutch nodded. "I just looked in the case."

"And that's *all* that's gone," Kilty said in a puzzled tone. "Not another thing in the place was touched."

"It doesn't figure," Dutch murmured.

"It certainly doesn't." Dr. Kilty straightened in his chair and said briskly, "Sergeant Barry has worked out last night's incident like this, Dutch. Just for your information. You're entitled to it, Barry says, because you paid for it with a crack on the skull. Anyway, these two thieves broke into the museum after dark—through the areaway window in one of our basement storage rooms. They came upstairs to the Egyptian wing, dodging Tom. They obviously didn't know *you* were here at all. They concealed themselves in the Egyptian wing after unscrewing the bulb in Tom's night light there. When Tom came in to investigate, they blackjacked him."

"Why? When they could have merely dodged him again, as they did getting up from the basement?"

"Because they intended to smash the Tut-ankh-amen display case, Barry thinks. And the crash of glass breaking would have made enough noise to draw Tom to the spot. And he might have prevented their getaway."

I see.

"They knocked Tom out. They were just going to start on the exhibit case, the sergeant surmises, when you came to the door of Egyptian Hall from your workroom and called to Tom. That's the first they knew you were there. They then simply repeated the tactics used on Tom. Only for you, the sight of Tom's unconscious head on the floor was the lure instead of a burned-out light bulb."

"Very smooth, weren't they, sir?"

"Very. Then they smashed the case. They took the Pharaoh's fingernail covers. They went calmly out to the lobby and escaped through the employees' door, failing to close it tightly behind them, so that it remained unlocked. On their way out they unscrewed the lobby night light. Just walked out."

"And nobody even laid a glove on them."

"Ah…yes, you might express it that way," Dr. Kilty said. His crimson sports jacket blazed in a streak of sunlight from the window. "But Sergeant Barry assures me the police will try very hard to locate them. He's coming to talk with you again, Dutch"—Dr. Kilty glanced at the clock on his wall—"in about half an hour."

Dutch nodded and sat there quietly for a moment, mulling over his superior's explanation. Then he said, "Dr. Kilty, the craziest thing is what they stole. They didn't even try for the petty cash. Just the set of false fingertips from King Tut's case."

"I agree. Five bits of gilt-covered lead with fake stones in them. What possible value could they have to anybody—except us?"

Dutch had relabeled the contents of that Tut-ankh-amen case only last week. He remembered the Pharaoh's fingertips perfectly—five pointed circlets, like tiny crowns, that glistened with a dull gold luster against their velvet nests in the display case. Each circlet had several rough-shaped studs of what looked like carnelian and turquoise set into it. These golden circlets had been worn on the ends of their fingers by the ancient Pharaohs—false fingernails, as it were, to give them chic and glitter at state banquets and ceremonials. And sometimes the Pharaohs were buried with their false fingertips in place.

Dutch thought about Tut-ankh-amen's tomb. In 1922, in the Valley of the Kings across the Nile from Luxor, the tomb of Pharaoh Tut-ankh-amen had been found with its contents intact and undamaged after more than thirty centuries underground. The fabulous treasures taken from the tomb—ranging from massive masks and mummy cases of pure thick gold to golden war chariots; from alabaster sculptures and likenesses of gods in precious metal to gold-sheathed furniture; from painted chests and delicate carvings to jewelry and serving bowls—proved so numerous, so costly, so unbelievably beautiful, that no other collection of antiquities anywhere equaled them in splendor or matched them in popular archaeological interest.

This entire treasure trove, with the exception of the Pharaoh's mummy in its golden outer case, was transferred to the National Museum in Cairo. Dutch knew that the five false fingertips in the Fulmer Museum, stolen last night by unknown men, were merely copies of some of the dazzling originals that had been found in the king's tomb and were now on display in the Cairo museum.

He answered Dr. Kilty's question with another. "Our fingernail covers *were* false, weren't they, sir? I mean, there's no chance they were valuable originals that actually came out of the king's tomb, is there?"

"Not a chance in the world. I personally ordered our copies made and supplied the color photographs they were modeled on. I supervised the work. No, our fingertips were made out of lead, sprayed with gilt paint. The carnelian and turquoise bosses in them weren't even genuine semiprecious stones. They're fakes, all right."

Dutch said, "And that's what makes it crazy for two guys to break into the museum just to steal them."

"Quite right. It is very puzzling."

"Maybe these fellows *thought* our fingernail covers were genuine antiquities. That they would be priceless."

"If so, you'd think some of our other exhibits would have tempted them, too. Yet they took only the fingertips."

"Small and easy to hide," Dutch speculated. "Easy to transport. If they thought they were real…"

Dr. Kilty stared at his desk and twitched his mustache. "Well, perhaps you've got a point. But with the genuine fingertips of Tut-ankh-amen on display in Cairo, any halfway intelligent thief would know…"

"Thieves aren't always smart, I guess," Dutch said. "At least, they're not supposed to be archaeologists or Egyptologists."

"I suppose not," said Kilty. Suddenly he slapped his desk with a sound like a pistol shot. "Wait!" he said in some excitement. "Four or five years ago, it seems to me, there *was* a theft reported from the Tut-ankh-amen collection in Cairo Museum! A number of valuable items were stolen."

"Were the Pharaoh's fingertips among them?" Dutch asked eagerly.

"I can't remember. I've got a list of the stolen items in the file, though, I'm pretty certain. It was circulated to all museums and collectors at the time, to warn them against acquiring the stolen antiquities even innocently." He rang a buzzer and his secretary promptly appeared from her tiny adjoining office.

"Yes, Dr. Kilty?"

"See if you can find me the list of items stolen from the National Museum in Cairo, Egypt, four or five years ago," he said. "I'm sure we kept it."

The secretary withdrew.

"Were the stolen articles ever recovered, sir?" Dutch inquired.

"Don't believe so, no."

"Then maybe," said Dutch, "these robbers of ours thought they were stealing genuine antiquities from us—antiquities they knew had already been stolen from Cairo."

"Let's wait until we see whether the fingertips were stolen," Dr. Kilty advised.

His secretary returned in a few moments with a mimeographed list several pages long. Dr. Kilty peered at it through his spectacles, then stabbed a finger at an item on the first page. "Here it is!" he barked. "Fingernail covers." He read from the description. "'Pointed circlets of pure gold, with studs of carnelian and turquoise, etc.,

etc. Five of these—a full set for one hand—were stolen out of a considerable number of similar fingertips found in King Tut-ankh-amen's tomb. The others are still in Cairo Museum, apparently."

"When?" asked Dutch.

"Four years ago this month," Dr. Kilty said. He put down the list and tapped his fingers on the desk top. "Very strange indeed. Five fingertips stolen from Cairo. Five stolen from us."

"So maybe ours *were* genuine!" Dutch exclaimed. "Maybe they were the originals that were stolen from the museum in Cano!"

Dr. Kilty shook his head. "Definitely not. I *know* ours were worthless copies. When you had them out of their case last week, relabeling them, I inspected them in your workroom when I checked your new labels. The gilt paint had worn thin on a couple of them. I could see the gray lead through the paint." He tilted his mustache in a broad smile of sympathy for Dutch's disappointment. "It would be a thrilling theory for you to go on," he said. "That our fingertips were the five stolen from Cairo. Originals that somehow got into our display case here in Riverlawn. But the Cairo theft and ours are mere coincidence, Dutch."

Dutch sighed. The very remote possibility that he might have been handling genuine golden fingertips from the hands of an emperor dead thirty-three centuries, had given him a shivery feeling down his spine for an instant. But he didn't doubt Dr. Kilty's statement for a moment. Dr. Kilty was an expert. If he said Fulmer Museum's fingertips were copies, they were copies. He stood up. "If that's all, sir, I'd better get back to work," he said. "I want to check the Karnak labeling I did last night with you before I send the captions out to the printer. And if Joe Barry's coming in a few minutes…"

"Yes, yes," Dr. Kilty said. "Glad you're all right, Dutch. Let's hope Sergeant Barry clears up our little mystery quickly. I'll see you later."

Dutch left the curator's office and went to his own workroom. He was tempted to tarry and tell Dr. Kilty that he now half believed he had seen his attacker of last night somewhere before. But he decided he'd tell Joe Barry first. He expected to be laughed at. And one laugher was enough.

* * * *

Sergeant Barry came into Dutch's workroom unannounced. He pulled up a straight chair beside the work table and said, "Morning, Dutch."

Dutch said, "Hi, Joe. What'll it be? Cherry sundae on chocolate as usual?"

Barry's eyes twinkled. "Make it two," he said. "I'm feeling in need of extra support today, somehow."

"What's the matter, Joe? Are you stymied already? My mother said to tell you she considers it a disgrace that you let things like this happen in a public museum." Dutch grinned at his friend.

"I let them happen! That's rich. What am I supposed to do? Keep a twenty-four hour watch on every building and every individual in town? You tell your mother, Dutch, that the police…"

"You *must* be stymied," Dutch said, "if you get so indignant over a gentle needling like that from my mother. Are you?"

Barry's expression softened. "We sure are. And that's the truth. We don't have a single little lead. We don't know who conked you and Tom Scott. We don't know what they wanted that made them risk a breaking and entering charge and two counts of aggravated assault. It certainly wasn't the ten dollars worth of lead and gilt in those phony fingertips of King Tut, I can tell you that. We don't know whether to look for local thugs or foreigners. We don't know what they look like except that one's tall and the other's short. We don't know where to start looking for them. And we couldn't identify them if we *could* find them. In fact, Dutch, you might say that as of right now, we don't know nothin'!"

Dutch grinned at him. Then, a little uneasily, he said, "I've got a lead for you, Joe."

Joe sat up straight. "A lead? That's more than Tom Scott could give us. Come on, Dutch. Out with it." Dutch sheepishly recounted to Sergeant Barry the incident of the TV repairman on the too-short step ladder. He took pains to describe as minutely as he could remember it his impression of hunched shoulders about both the TV man and the man who had blackjacked him last night. He gave Barry as thorough a word picture of the TV man as he possibly could, describing his clothes, his facial characteristics, his semibaldness, his dark glasses—everything that might help Barry to identify him.

As he told it to Joe, the story sounded very thin indeed to Dutch—an insubstantial suggestion of similarity between two strange men that wasn't strong enough or definite enough to base even an obscure hunch on. But he went doggedly ahead with his recital. "It probably means nothing at all, Joe," he finished lamely, "but the guy that hit me last night *did* seem faintly familiar. And the only reason I can think of for *why* he did is because the TV man who came to my house by mistake several weeks ago carried his shoulders the same way."

"Don't apologize," Barry said, busily making notes in a small blue-bound book he took from his pocket. "You're the only spot of brightness in what has been so far a bleak and lousy day. This lead of yours isn't much, Dutch, but it's at least better than the real nothing we had before. Thanks. I'll get on it right away."

"What'll you do?" Dutch couldn't help asking.

"Check out the TV repair places in town, first. Find any new men recently added to their service crews. Get you to identify the right guy when we find him. Then put him and his record through the grinder. What else? If he turns out to be a noble character with an unshakable alibi for last night at ten o'clock, we'll know he's just what he says he is: a TV repairman who went to the wrong address. If, on the other hand, he *hasn't* got an unshakable alibi, he might turn out to be a nasty museum robber and boy slugger. See what I mean? Routine investigation, Dutch."

Dutch cleared his throat. "If you find him, will I hear from you?"

"You'll hear from me," Sergeant Barry promised.

CHAPTER 6

The Meeting at Costello's

The next day was Saturday. Dutch worked at the museum until noon. When he got home, he found Cam sitting comfortably in his living room before the TV set, waiting for him.

"Hiya, Dutch," Cam said. "Poor hard-working fellow. I slept till eleven this morning. Aren't you envious? A man ought to get all day Saturday off, I say."

"You get it off," Dutch retorted with a grin, "and what do you do with it? Sleep! A waste of time. I've already put in a good half day's work. So now I can relax with a clear conscience. Why are you here?"

"I thought we might watch the American-Russian track meet on TV. If you have no better suggestion, of course."

"Good idea. How long have you been waiting for me?"

"Half an hour. But Hilda kept me entertained. She seems too bright for a freshman, Dutch, you know that?"

"Hilda? She's bright in everything but domestic science. In cooking she falls flat on her face."

"That's funny. She's out in the kitchen now, baking a batch of cookies for us to eat while we watch the track meet."

Dutch stared. "Cooking?" He laughed, guessing that his sister, romantically inclined toward Cam, was trying to impress the big fellow with her cooking skill. He was about to say, "If Hilda makes cookies, it'll be with store-bought cookie mix," but then, moved by loyalty to his sister, he sniffed and said instead, "Say, something does smell pretty good, at that!"

They settled down comfortably to watch the track meet. In a few minutes Hilda came in with a plate of chocolate chip cookies, still warm from the oven. As Cam thanked her for them she gave him a melting look, tossed her head at Dutch, who winked at her, then left them alone again.

They had finished the cookies fifteen minutes later when the telephone rang. Hilda answered it in the dining room.

"It's for you," she told Dutch. "Sergeant Barry."

Dutch spoke briefly into the instrument. Cam and Hilda heard him say, "Sure, sure, I can come now. How about Cam Osborn? Can he come, too? He might drive me over in his car."

When he hung up, Dutch said to Cam in an excited voice, "Joe Barry wants me to take a look at a TV repairman he's nosed out and see if it's the guy I told you about with the short ladder. Want to come along?"

"Do I?" Cam rose with alacrity. "I wouldn't miss it."

"Please, Cam," Hilda said, fluffing her hair self-consciously, "take care of my brother. He's likely to get hit on the head when he's out alone."

Cam laughed. "Trust me, Hilda," he said. "I'll look out for him. Thanks for the cookies."

Hilda blushed.

* * * *

Dutch and Cam lost no time in driving to police headquarters. They asked the desk sergeant for Sergeant Barry and were sent into Joe's first-floor cubbyhole of an office at once.

"Dutch," Barry said when the boys were seated, "I haven't had much luck with the TV repairman lead you gave me. I've checked out all the TV services and service shops in town. Only one of them—Costello's—has hired a new repairman within the last month. And he doesn't match too closely your description of the man who came to your house, apparently. He's a bare possibility, though. In fact, the only one. So I thought you ought to have a look at him, just to make absolutely sure he can be eliminated. Costello's records show no call for TV aerial repair at your house on the afternoon in question. No record of any service call at one-o-four Seventh Street, either, for that afternoon at any TV service shop in town. But the new man working for Costello is kind of tall and thin and half bald, and he wears a baseball cap on the job, according to his boss. I want you to look at him and see if you can identify him as your TV repairman. Okay?"

"Sure," Dutch agreed. "Let's go."

Barry drove them to Costello's TV Repair on Main Street in a police cruiser.

"This repairman's name is Jablonsky," Joe Barry told Dutch as he parked the cruiser at the curb. "When he appears, take a good look at him. If he looks familiar, try not to let on to him. All set?"

Dutch nodded. He and Cam followed Sergeant Barry into the TV service shop. New and used TV sets crowded the small room. A man stood pensively behind a battered counter at the back of the store.

"Yes?" he said.

"I'm Sergeant Barry, Riverlawn police," Barry said, showing his badge. "I called you this morning about your man Jablonsky."

"Yeah," Costello said. "What's he done?"

"Nothing, probably," said Barry, smiling. "I don't want to alarm him, or you either. I just want this boy, Dutch Schildecker, to take a look at him, if it's all right with you. Is he here now?"

"Yeah. In the shop out back. Shall I call him? You can look at him all you please, as far as I'm concerned. But I hope he's clean. He's the best repairman I've been able to hire for three years. I wouldn't want to lose him less'n a month after I got him."

"Call him in here, please," Barry requested.

Costello raised his voice and bellowed through a door beside the counter. "Jablonsky! Front and center! Friends of yours to see you!"

They heard heavy footsteps approaching, then a man appeared in the doorway. He was clad in blue jeans and a dark blue shirt open at the throat. A baseball cap perched askew on his head. His hands were dirty. So was his face. Costello's hail had evidently interrupted him in the middle of a repair job, for he still held a screwdriver in one hand.

He blinked pale eyes and said, "Friends of mine?" His gaze rested on Barry, Dutch, and Cam.

"Aren't you the Jablonsky that used to go with my sister-in-law's niece in Otterbon?" Joe Barry said, holding out his hand. "She told me to look you up. Maronic is her name. Lily Maronic."

Jablonsky came into the front room and stood beside Costello behind the counter. His dour face showed puzzlement. He lifted off his baseball cap and scratched his head. "Otterbon?" he asked.

"Where's that?" He shrugged. "I never heard of the place. Never knew a dame called Lily, either."

Dutch stared fixedly at Jablonsky while Barry kept him engaged in conversation. The man was medium tall and rather thin. He was half-bald, as Joe had said. But his shoulders, far from being hunched up, were sharply sloping. And his hair was a dull blond, not brown.

After a quick glance at Dutch, Joe Barry said apologetically to Jablonsky, "I guess Lily and I got our wires crossed somehow. I'm sorry to bother you. You're not the right man, that's plain. Must be some other Jablonsky in town."

"There ain't any other," Jablonsky said. He turned unhurriedly and went out of sight through the door into the workshop, muttering, "Crazy people!"

Costello grinned. "He wouldn't be likely to have friends in Otterbon, Sergeant. Or any place else. He's kind of antisocial. But a dam good repairman all the same."

"Thanks for your help, Mr. Costello," Barry said then. "Come on, boys."

They went out to the sidewalk and climbed into the police car in silence. Joe switched on the ignition. Then he said quietly to Dutch, "Well?"

Dutch shook his head. "That's not the man, Joe," he declared. "Not the TV man who came to our place."

"You sure?"

"Absolutely. This guy is different in any number of ways. Different hair color. Different shoulders. Not tall enough. Different voice. Everything."

"I was afraid of that," Barry said reluctantly. "So there goes our only faint lead in the museum robbery."

"I was pretty sure it wouldn't amount to anything. I told you so, remember?"

"I remember. But a cop can always hope, can't he?" Joe threw the cruiser into gear. "Well, back to the mines, boys."

Cam, who hadn't uttered a word throughout their visit to Costello's, spoke up now from the back seat of the police car. "The ladder," he said in a thoughtful voice.

"The ladder? What about the ladder?" Barry asked.

"It points to a truck," Cam suggested. "Dutch's fake TV man, if he was a fake, and I guess he was, must have had a truck to carry that extension ladder to Dutch's house."

"I couldn't see his truck from my window," Dutch reminded Cam.

"I know it. But *if* the TV man was a phony, then he'd have to get a truck and ladder somewhere, don't you see? To support his TV masquerade. So maybe he stole somebody else's truck and ladder."

"It's a thought," Barry said. "We'll take a look in the book when we get back to headquarters."

* * * *

Back at headquarters Barry left them sitting in his tiny office while he went off to consult the police daybook for the day when Dutch had been awakened by the TV man and his ladder. During his absence Cam said, "It's a foolish idea, maybe, Dutch, but if we could find out that somebody had his truck and ladder stolen that day, then we'd be real sure that your TV man was a phony. And that he was up to some monkey business at your house, just as he was at the museum. If it's the same guy, of course."

"A big 'if'," Dutch said disconsolately. "I'm not at all sure of my brain wave about the hunched shoulders, Cam. I told Joe that."

"Well," said Cam, "at least playing detective like this is the most fun we've had since the water main broke in the chemistry lab last year."

Dutch felt his spirits lift. "That's right. Although I'd just as soon not have to get slugged in the head again very soon. *That* wasn't fun."

Sergeant Barry came into the room. He patted Cam's shoulder. "You got an instinct for this work, Cam," he said. "You're right. Jesse Swain, a house painter near city line, had his truck stolen from in front of his house the morning of that Saturday, complete with one two-section extension ladder strapped on top. He reported it missing as soon as he discovered the theft. But before suppertime the same day he called again and reported the truck and ladder were back in front of his house, unharmed. So we canceled it off our books."

Cam, feeling quite proud of himself, smiled. "Well, then," he asked, "What's the next step?"

"Next step?"

"Yeah. Now that we know Dutch's man was a fake for sure, and stole a truck and ladder, where do we go from here?"

"Nowhere," said Barry quietly. "I'm sorry, boys. But this new bit of knowledge doesn't seem to help us much with the main question. Or two main questions, rather. First, was your fake TV man the same man you thought you recognized in the museum the other night, Dutch? And second, if he was, how do we go about finding him?"

"I see what you mean." Dutch sighed. "The whole TV angle is washed up as a possible line of investigation since Jablonsky turned out to be okay?"

"That's about it, I'm afraid. I'm sorry, Dutch. But I won't slack up on the other lines of investigation. I want to get those museum thieves. Not because they stole some worthless Egyptian fingertips, but because they manhandled you and Tom Scott. Your mother's pretty much right, you know. We shouldn't allow things like that to happen in Riverlawn. And we're not going to give up easy on this one."

"I'll tell Mother what you said," Dutch replied with a smile.

"And try to think of something else about your impressions of the museum robbery that might prove helpful to us, will you?"

"Sure. I'll do my best."

Barry stood up. "Great," he said. "Thanks for your cooperation on Jablonsky. I'm as disappointed as you are that it turned out to be wasted effort, believe me. But that's what ninety-nine percent of police work is."

Dutch hesitated for a moment before he, too, rose from his chair. "Joe," he said then, "I don't know what this is all about, and I don't know who is at the bottom of it, but I do feel that something involving me personally is going on. Something pretty serious. And pretty dangerous, too, if getting knocked cold the other night is any sign."

"So?" said Barry, nodding.

"So I don't worry too much about myself," Dutch said slowly. "I'll keep my eyes peeled. But I don't want to take any chances of having Mother and Hilda mixed up in it, whatever it is. They might get hurt. And I certainly don't want that to happen."

"I don't either. But I honestly believe, since Jablonsky failed us, that the museum robbery and your TV man episode are two unrelated incidents, Dutch. You *happened* to be home early from your track meet the first day and accidentally interrupted a perfectly routine burglary attempt. You *happened* to be in the museum working late and accidentally got conked by thieves with no personal malice."

"I hope you're right," Dutch said, rubbing the side of his head reminiscently.

"What I'll do, though," Barry promised, "is to have the crew of police car seventeen that covers your neighborhood keep an extra close watch on your house. How's that?"

"That's fine," said Dutch with relief. "Thanks a lot, Joe."

"For nothing," Barry said. "Let me hear if anything else occurs to you. Right?"

"Right."

Dutch and Cam left his office.

CHAPTER 7

Hilda Points the Way

They drove back to Dutch's house in Cam's jalopy.

It was four o'clock. The Russian-American track meet they'd been watching on television before Barry's call was long since over. So the boys sat at the curb in the jalopy for a few minutes, discussing their recent taste of police work.

"You're certain Jablonsky isn't the TV repairman who came to your house?" Cam asked.

"Sure, I'm certain! You think I wouldn't have known him today if he'd been the same person?"

"It stands to reason you would," Cam admitted. "But the guy had on dark glasses that day, remember. Maybe they'd change his appearance enough to fool you."

"Huh-uh," Dutch said positively. "Not a Chinaman's chance. It just wasn't Jablonsky, that's all." They sat in silence for a moment, busy with their thoughts. Then Dutch said, "Joe Barry seems convinced that there's no connection between the TV man and the museum robbery, now that Jablonsky turned out to be a false lead."

"Yeah. And he could be right. It makes sense that way."

"Not to me, it doesn't. There's too much coincidence in this mess, Cam. Look. Somebody went to the trouble of stealing a truck and ladder so he could rob *my* house, despite the fact that we haven't anything in the place worth stealing. Then somebody broke into the museum where *I* work and knocked *me* out while committing another burglary. And I even have the feeling that I recognized the same man in both cases! Maybe I'm wrong about that. But even so, I still think there's something going on that involves me personally."

"If you feel that way about it," Cam said loyally, "I'm with you. You aren't any dreamer, pal, I'm sure of that. So if you say some crook is focusing on you, let him focus on me, too. We can probably handle him between us." Cam made a muscle with his right arm. Then he slapped Dutch on the back.

Dutch laughed. "Thanks for joining me in the target area, old buddy. Have you had any good blackjack blows lately? They're all the rage now, you know."

Cam was immediately contrite. "I was just laughing it up, Dutch," he apologized. "I wasn't belittling the danger you're in, believe me."

"I know." Dutch stared through the slanting windshield of the jalopy. "I keep thinking about that TV man, Cam. And I keep thinking that there's something connected with him that I ought to remember."

Cam grinned. "Hunched shoulders, no doubt."

"No. Something else."

Cam said, "The way you told it to me that Saturday night at Cox's, the man woke you up with his ladder thumping against the house, said he was supposed to examine your aerial, and claimed he had a wrong address when you told him your aerial was okay."

Dutch started. "Wrong address!" he exclaimed. "That's it, Cam! When he said, 'Isn't this Seventh Street?' he took a piece of paper out of his pocket to check the address. Or at least I thought that's what he was doing."

"Yeah. I remember you mentioned that to me. What about it?"

"Well, he dropped the paper when he was trying to stuff it back into his pocket!"

Cam's blue eyes began to sparkle. "And he didn't pick it up when he got down off the ladder?"

"I don't think so. I don't think he even noticed that he dropped it."

"And if he didn't pick it up when he got down off the ladder, it ought to be there still?"

"Right!" Dutch scrambled out of the jalopy like a man who has suddenly discovered he is sitting on a snake. Cam leaped after him.

"Come on!" Dutch yelled, running for the back of the house. "It ought to be under my bedroom window!"

But it wasn't.

Quartering the area like two beagles eager to put up birds, the boys searched every inch of ground under Dutch's bedroom window. The lawn back there was patchy and the grass dry and faded, but any scrap of paper more than an inch square should have been instantly visible upon it.

They went over the ground a second time, careful to miss no single possible hiding place, but without success.

"Darn it!" Dutch said in dismay, "I was sure he dropped that paper here!"

Cam looked up as Hilda's voice reached them from the back door. "What are you two *doing* out there?" she called curiously. "Crawling around on your hands and knees like…like bears! Have you lost something, Dutch?"

"Yes," Dutch said, "But you wouldn't be interested, Hilda. Nothing important."

"Well," Hilda replied, "maybe I could help you look for it if you told me what it was."

"It was a piece of paper, that's all," said Dutch shortly.

"How big?" Hilda's eyes were on Cam's reclining figure, now stretched lazily on the grass.

Dutch showed her with his hands.

"How long ago did you lose it?" Hilda persisted.

"What difference does that make? Several weeks ago, anyway. It isn't here."

"Well, I just wanted to tell you I have another plate of cookies, if you and Cam would like them," Hilda said with a sidelong glance at Cam.

"Ah!" Cam beamed at her. "I can't say No to cookies!"

"Wait a minute then." They heard her bustling about in the kitchen. When she emerged from the back door carrying the cookies, she said, "Maybe the rain melted it."

Cam bit into a cookie. "Melted what?" he mumbled with his mouth full.

"The piece of paper you're looking for."

"Are you out of your mind?" Dutch spoke up, helping himself to a cookie. "It hasn't rained for a month. Anyway, rain doesn't melt…"

Hilda interrupted him. "Then maybe you cut it up with the lawn mower last Saturday," she said primly, "when you mowed the lawn."

Squinting against the westering sun, Dutch said, "I did cut the grass at that. But I didn't see the paper. And I would have if it was here."

"These cookies are really great, Hilda!" Cam said with enthusiasm. He sampled another.

"Thanks," said Hilda. She lingered in the backyard long enough to say, "Even if it hasn't rained since you lost your old paper, Dutch, it *was* awfully windy a couple of weeks ago one clay when that branch blew off our elm tree out front. Maybe the wind blew your paper away." With this parting shot she disappeared into the kitchen.

Cam sat up. "Say," he began, "your sister may have something there…"

"I should have thought of that myself," Dutch grunted in disgust. He stood up and started for the privet hedge that bordered the eastern edge of the small backyard.

Cam followed him. Together they scanned the ground along the privet stems, peering under the bushy hedge.

They saw the scrap of paper at the same instant.

"There!" Cam said.

"Here!" Dutch said, reaching for it with an eager hand. When he picked it up, he cast a hasty glance at the kitchen window to see if Hilda was watching. She wasn't in sight.

"I told you she was pretty bright for a freshman," Cam said with undisguised delight. "What's the paper got on it? Anything?"

"Something," Dutch said, smoothed out the crumpled scrap. "But what?"

They stared at the six-inch piece of weather-marked paper. It was obviously the top left corner of a letterhead-sized sheet, torn off jaggedly. It bore six lines of writing in purplish ink. First, three lines of lettering, followed by a dash and then the cryptic notation "1A2F3W." Then came a space. Then another three lines of writing followed by a dash and the first two digits of what seemed to be another letter-figure combination like the first—"IB/." The paper had been torn from the sheet right through the middle of this terminal combination, however, so the final four digits were missing.

Dutch and Cam frowned at the paper. "This can't be that TV man's paper," Dutch said finally. "And if it is, what's it mean?"

"Don't ask me," Cam replied. "You're supposed to be the egg-head of this team, remember?"

For although the figure-letter combinations at the end of each three-line notation were plain enough to the boys, the six lines of writing on the paper were not.

Those six lines were written in a foreign language that neither Dutch nor Cam had ever seen before.

* * * *

"It looks like a list," Dutch offered. They were back in Cam's jalopy, sitting in front of Dutch's house, scrutinizing the torn scrap of paper with undiminished bewilderment. "Let's not go into the house," Dutch had suggested, "or Hilda will drive us nuts with questions once she gets a glimpse of this crazy thing."

"Maybe she could read it," Cam laughed. "She found it for us, after all."

They agreed, however, that not even Hilda could make anything of the foreign writing. The rough, hand-written letters weren't familiar in the least. "It's Oriental," Dutch said. "At least it's got little marks and curlicues and dots and stuff in it like Japanese or Siamese, or something. Look at that."

"Maybe it's Russian!" Cam suddenly came alive at the thought that they might be mixed up in a spy case. International intrigue stories were his favorite reading next to sports stories.

"It isn't Russian," Dutch said, shaking his head. "I've seen what Russian looks like. Anyway, you know, Cam, that even if we could read it, it might not mean a thing. The chances are it's not the paper the TV man dropped at all. Maybe it's just a piece of an old love letter written to somebody's foreign maid or something."

"That's a likely theory. Or a piece out of the Afghanistan Navy's Code Book."

"Afghanistan hasn't got a navy."

"See what I mean? It could be anything."

"It looks like a list of some kind."

"So suppose it's a list. A list of what?"

Dutch shrugged. "Oh, people, or things of some kind, or…"

Cam grinned at his friend. "That's brilliant, that is," he said pityingly. "Why don't we concentrate on the part we can read? Those figures and letters at the end of the lines."

"Okay with me."

"All right. I'm concentrating. Are you?"

"Hard. 1A2F3W."

"Does anything come through?"

"Not a thing. I'm blank as an empty cartridge."

"Me too."

They sat in companionable silence for five minutes. Cam turned on his pocket radio and got some quiet orchestral music. "To help me concentrate," he explained.

At length Dutch said, "Maybe we ought to show this paper to Joe Barry. It's possible, after all, that it is the paper my fake TV man dropped. So it could be a clue. And joe asked us to tell him if we thought of anything else that might help."

"Joe's not too keen on the TV-man angle now," Cam said. "Besides, old Joe couldn't read this paper any more than we can. What we need here, my friend, is a foreign language expert."

"You're probably right."

"So who's a foreign language expert? Do we know any?"

"Not for this queer-type language. If it was French or German or Latin or Spanish or something like that, we could ask one of the teachers at school."

"I'm still in favor of asking Hilda," said Cam. "There's a bright kid."

"Strictly a baby sister," said Dutch absently. "Only fourteen." He looked glumly out the window. "Maybe we should just forget all about the stupid piece of paper."

"It isn't helping us much yet," Cam replied, "but it might, if we could only read what it says. There ought to be *somebody* in Riverlawn who could translate it for us.

All at once Dutch snapped his fingers. "Sure!" he exclaimed. "There is! Dr. Kilty. My boss. If you can read Egyptian hieroglyphics, you can read anything! How about that?"

"Now you're talking sense," Cam said. He leaned forward and turned the key in the ignition switch of the old Chevy. "Where's he live?"

"Hold it!" Dutch grinned. "We don't have to see him this minute! I'll show him the paper when I go to work on Monday. It's not that important."

"Well, then, my romantic friend," suggested Cam, racing his engine in neutral, "how about going with me to gather up Kathy and then stopping in to do a little Saturday shopping in Wexler's Gift Shop? I understand a certain blonde Janet is stunning the customers there this season."

"This," agreed Dutch readily, "sounds like the kind of Saturday afternoon work I like to do! Drive on, MacDuff."

CHAPTER 8

The Scrap of Paper

On Monday morning Dutch arrived at the museum ten minutes ahead of the official opening hour. He had planned, if Dr. Kilty was also an early arrival at his office, to consult the museum curator about the puzzling scrap of paper he and Cam had found under the hedge on Saturday afternoon.

Dr. Kilty, however, far from being early, was an hour late in getting to the museum. His delay, as he graphically explained upon arrival, was due to an unexpected puncture in one of his tires. He'd had to change the wheel himself, and had found the mysteries of how a modern jack operates almost impenetrable.

Consequently it was eleven-thirty before Dutch had an opportunity to talk with Dr. Kilty. And by that time Dutch had almost decided not to talk with him at all. For the more he pondered it, the more unlikely it seemed to Dutch that the scrap of paper could really be a clue to the mystery of the TV man and the theft of the false fingertips. Wasn't it straining credulity too far to believe that a few lines of foreign writing on a torn paper found under a hedge could have any connection whatever with Dutch or with Fulmer Memorial Museum? Dutch was inclined to think so.

Nevertheless, when Dr. Kilty called him into his office to discuss the relabeling of the museum's exhibit of wall reliefs from the Mastaba of Ti at Sakkara, Dutch determined to ask the curator's advice.

Dr. Kilty, as it turned out, made it easy for Dutch; the curator himself brought up the matter.

"Well, Dutch," he said, "no ill effects from your experience last week, I trust?"

"I feel great," Dutch answered. "How about Tom Scott?"

"He's all right, too. He'll be back on the job tonight. But Sergeant Barry tells me there's no great progress being made in catching our thieves."

"No, sir. Did Sergeant Barry tell you about my fake TV repairman and Jablonsky?"

The curator nodded. "Yes. Too bad it didn't work out, Dutch. Do you still think there's a possibility your TV man and our museum robber are one and the same?"

"I'm not sure, sir. Sergeant Barry doesn't think so."

"I know. He's doing what he can along other lines, though. Checking what all our local…ah…malefactors were doing at ten o'clock last Thursday night. Covering pawnshops and other places where our stolen fingertips might turn up. And so forth."

"If the thieves think the fingertips are genuine," Dutch said, "collectors of antiquities would be a better bet for their disposal than pawnshops."

"Agreed. Barry is aware of that, of course."

"I suppose so."

"Barry hasn't a single lead, Dutch. He's floundering, groping in the dark. When your TV clue petered out on him, I never saw such a discouraged policeman. He likes you. And he wants to find the men who slugged you, as well as solve our museum robbery. You haven't thought of anything else that might prove helpful to him, have you?"

Dutch pulled his wallet out of his hip pocket and removed from it the scrap of paper he and Cam had found in his backyard. Carefully and without words, he unfolded it, smoothed it out on Dr. Kilty's desk top, and pushed it over to him. Then he said, "I don't think so, sir. Cam Osborn and I were still trying to tie my TV man into it Saturday, even though Sergeant Barry no longer believes him significant. And we found this scrap of paper in my backyard. There's a bare possibility the TV man may have dropped it. Can you read what it says, sir?"

Dr. Kilty bent his head and examined the scrap of paper through his spectacles. Dutch held his breath.

"Looks like part of a list of something," Dr. Kilty said at length.

"We thought so, too," Dutch said eagerly. "But can you read the language, sir?"

The curator shook his head. "I'm sorry. I can't." A tilt of his mustache signaled a smile. "And I'm rather embarrassed to admit it, I might add."

Dutch's heart sank with disappointment. "Why?" he inquired.

"Because," said Dr. Kilty, "as a man more than superficially familiar with ancient Egyptian writing, I feel somewhat ashamed at my lack of proficiency in the modern language of the country."

"Is that what it is?" Dutch asked. "Arabic?"

"That's what it is. I recognize it, but I can't translate it, Dutch. I'm sorry."

Dutch sat back in his chair. "I guess it doesn't make any difference, sir. Probably nothing to do with our robbery, anyhow."

The curator continued to look at the paper. "Still," he said thoughtfully, "it's odd, in a way, that a notation in Arabic should turn up here in Riverlawn in a case involving Egyptian antiquities."

Dutch kept quiet.

"And in your backyard, at that, Dutch, where you interrupted a fraudulent TV repairman trying to burgle your house. You say you think the TV man dropped this scrap of paper?"

"We can't be sure after all this time. But I think he dropped something, and this could be it. It's possible, that's all."

Kilty looked up from the paper. "How did he speak, this fake TV man of yours? With a noticeable accent, or in colloquial American?"

"There was something a little funny about his talk," Dutch replied. "Kind of as though he wasn't too sure of his American slang. But that's all."

"Could he have been an Arab by any chance?"

"An Arab?" Dutch laughed. "I never talked to an Arab or even saw one, except on TV and at the movies, so I don't know. But I'd guess not. This guy was strictly American, I'd say—maybe with foreign parents. But I don't really know."

Kilty tilted his mustache and said, "You can't tell the Arab without his burnoose, is that it?"

"I can't tell an Arab *with* his burnoose."

Dr. Kilty studied the scrap of paper again. "These notations at the end of the third and sixth lines aren't Arabic. They're straightforward English."

Dutch grinned and said disarmingly, "The letters are English, sir, but I always understood figures like that *were* Arabic numerals."

Dr. Kilty laughed aloud. "*Touché*, Dutch!" He slapped the paper. "Any ideas about these English letters and *Arabic* numerals, then?"

"Not a single idea, sir."

"Well," Dr. Kilty said, looking at his wrist watch, "are you planning to show this to Sergeant Barry?"

Dutch hesitated. "No, sir," he said at length. "Not unless you think it's a bona fide clue this time. I gave Joe a bad steer, I suppose, with that TV man resemblance, and I don't want to repeat my mistake. It causes him nothing but useless trouble."

"I can sympathize with your reluctance. And I agree, upon deliberation, that it does seem to be reaching pretty far to attach any significance to your scrap of paper. But…"

"I'd almost decided not even to show it to you, sir."

"No, no. I want you to come to me at any time, Dutch. You know that. I only wish I could read your writing for you."

"Is there anybody in town who can?" Dutch asked.

"Of course!" Dr. Kilty brightened. "I'm sure the Bertrand Language School on Garden Street would have a staff member who can read Arabic. Why not try them?"

"I will," said Dutch. "And thank you, sir."

"Wait a minute." Kilty picked up his telephone and asked his secretary to get him the Bertrand School on the wire. When she did, he confirmed the presence of an Arabic-speaking teacher on their staff and arranged for Dutch to drop in at his lunch-hour to see him.

Dutch walked the five blocks to Garden Street, stopping on the way at his winter employer, Cox's, to eat a hurried sandwich washed down with a strawberry milkshake.

The Bertrand Language School was located in a square, tan brick residence converted twenty years before into a combination school-and-office building. A brass plaque beside the front door bore the legend:

BERTRAND LANGUAGE SCHOOL
All Modern Languages Taught

Dutch went into the foyer and approached a receptionist sitting at a small desk there. "I'm Dutch Schildecker," he introduced himself. "Dr. Kilty, the curator of Fulmer Memorial Museum, called you a while ago about somebody who could read an Arabic inscription for me."

"Yes, Mr. Schildecker, sit down over there, if you please. I'll call our Mr. Petri." She muttered into her telephone for a moment, then smiled brightly at Dutch and said, "he'll be right down. He's busy teaching, but he says he can spare a minute."

"Thank you." Dutch sat down in a contour chair near her desk, crossed his legs, and tried to hide his nervousness. He couldn't quite rid himself of the feeling that he was making a fool of himself over this silly scrap of paper.

He didn't have long to wait. A short, bristle-haired man with enormous bags under his eyes and a large gold signet ring on his left hand came bustling in from a corridor to the receptionist's right and raised his eyebrows at her. "Where's Mr. Schildecker?" he asked. "I thought you said…"

The receptionist frowned at him and motioned to Dutch with her head. "Here's Mr. Schildecker," she said. "This is Mr. Petri, Mr. Schildecker."

Petri swung around to Dutch in some confusion and said, "How do you do? I was expecting an older person, somehow. Are you the man Dr. Kilty called about?"

"Yes," said Dutch. He went right to the point. "Can you read Arabic, Mr. Petri?"

"Certainly. Arabic is one of the seven languages I am qualified to teach."

"Swell," said Dutch, pulling out his piece of paper. "This is the Arabic writing I'd like to get translated, please." He held it out. "Will you charge much for the job?"

The language teacher smiled, elongating the bags under his eyes by the horizontal pressure. "Depends on how much of a job it is," he replied. He looked down at the scrap of paper in Dutch's hand and laughed. "This is nothing," he said then. "I'll do it for free, young man. Won't take a minute. Here." He grabbed the scrap of paper, walked over to the receptionist's desk, borrowed a pencil and piece of typewriter paper from her, and wrote busily for two minutes, consulting Dutch's Arabic original at frequent intervals.

Dutch, who had arisen at Petri's entrance, stood awkwardly in the middle of the foyer, watching him. Nothing, Dutch thought to himself. The guy said this is nothing the second he looked at the Arabic. He'll think I'm some kind of a nut, coming here to bother him with a crazy scrap of paper. Probably turn out to be a laundry ticket or something.

Mr. Petri whirled around, handed Dutch his scrap of paper and the sheet on which he had scrawled the translation, and waved a hand negligently when Dutch expressed his gratitude. Then he went off into the corridor, saying over his shoulder, "No trouble at all, son. Send your friends to Bertrand School if they want to learn languages!"

Dutch didn't hear him.

He was staring down in astonishment at Mr. Petri's translation from the Arabic.

* * * *

"You could have knocked me down with a powder puff," Dutch told Cam that night. "I looked at this translation, Cam, and I could hardly believe my own eyes!"

"Well, come on!" urged Cam impatiently. "You're killing me with all this suspense. What did the Arabic say?"

They were sprawled side by side on the sofa in Dutch's living room, their legs stretched far out before them, sitting, as Dutch's mother expressed it, "on the backs of their necks." Hilda was visiting her friend Rita on the next street; Mrs. Schildecker was in the basement putting a load of laundry through the automatic washing machine.

Dutch said, "I'll give you three guesses."

"A list of…let's see…dry-cleaning establishments in Casablanca?"

"That's one wrong."

"A list of best-sellers from the Cairo *Gazette*?"

"Two wrong."

"Algerian movie stars' addresses?"

"You're getting warm with the address pitch," Dutch said. "There were two names and two addresses in Arabic on that little scrap of paper. And what do you think the first name and address was?"

Cam said, "Do I have to choke it out of you by main force, little man?"

Dutch shook his head, smiling. "Nope. Here it is, Sherlock. Take a look at the translation for yourself." He held out the penciled translation sheet to Cam.

Cam jerked it out of his hand and scanned it at a glance. His mouth opened in surprise. He turned to his friend and said in a dumfounded voice, "Is this a gag?"

"No gag. I wish it were." Together they gazed at the words Mr. Petri had written down:

Oscar Schildecker
Seventeenth Street
Riverlawn, Pa. 1A2F3W

Natalie R. Cosgrove Lake Drive
Conawachie, N. Y. IB

"How about that for a piece of Arabic prose?" Dutch finally asked with assumed lightness.

Out of sheer amazement Cam used his strongest oath: "May I be dipped in whale oil!" he muttered. "Unless these old eyes deceive me, that first name is Oscar Schildecker."

"That's me, pal."

"It is. And this *proves* there was some personal element in that TV mans attempted burglary, wouldn't you say? The guy had your name and address in his shirt pocket! In Arabic!"

"I've thought plenty about what it could mean," Dutch said. "And I'm still away out in left field. But that much is right—the TV man had this specific house in mind that day. His story about the wrong address—Seventh Street instead of Seventeenth—must have been just a quick cover-up he tried on the spur of the moment when I surprised him by being at home."

"Yeah. Must have been."

"This," said Dutch, "is the time for Osborn to use that big brilliant brain of his once more."

"True. True. Do you happen to have a coke in the house? I think better when I'm swallowing, somehow."

Dutch grinned. "No coke. You'll just have to think on an empty stomach."

"Well, that's pretty rough. Nero Wolfe eats like a horse and drinks gallons of beer while deducing. But I'll do the best I can."

"Good," said Dutch. "So get started."

"First," said Cam, dropping his bantering manner, "I'd say that this pretty well nails down three things: that your TV man *was* phony; that he wasn't just trying any old burglary but was interested in your particular house; and that he either reads Arabic or is an Arab, or both."

"I'm with you so far. No argument."

"Okay. So second, he was after something special in your house—something he knew was here, or thought was here."

"Check again."

"And third, what was the something special he was after?" Cam looked at Dutch. "The big question. Any ideas? It's your house, buddy."

"Not the faintest."

"You don't ever keep any of the museum exhibits at home, do you?"

"Nope. And I wasn't even working at the museum yet when the TV man was here."

"That's right."

"Besides, I certainly didn't have those Egyptian fingernail covers lying around the house. And that was the only thing my TV man—if it was my TV man—stole from the museum."

"You still think it was the same man?"

"I sure do, after finding this address list. But Joe Barry doesn't. So this scrap of paper we found won't mean a thing to him as far as the museum robbery's concerned. And that's the only real crime that's been committed so far, remember."

"Your TV man swiped a truck. That's a crime."

"Yeah, I forgot that. But he only borrowed it."

Cam sat silently contemplating the translation of the Arabic. At length he said, "Where would he get your name? It's screwy. Did you ever know any Arabs, Dutch?"

"Not one. Never even saw one in my life except in the movies."

"And *Oscar* Schildecker! Your right name. This Arab ladder-bug even knows your secrets."

"I've been wondering about that, too."

"Hey!" Cam sat up straight on the sofa and slammed his big fist down on the arm. "I have an idea!"

"Good," said Dutch. "If we ever needed one, we need it now."

"Your father," said Cam. "His name was Oscar Schildecker, too! Right?"

"Right. I was Junior. But I dropped the Junior."

"So maybe this name in Arabic isn't yours, son. Maybe it's your *father's* name!"

"Say! That could be it. Somebody might not know my father is dead."

Cam got up and walked back and forth in excitement. "You know what we've got now?" he asked. "We've got a whole new field of speculation to mess around in!"

Dutch heard his mother come up from the basement into the kitchen. "Mom!" he called to her. "Can you come in here for a second?" He paused. "Cam thinks this may be *Dad's* name on the paper and not mine at all!"

Mrs. Schildecker came in and said hello to Cam. She looked thin and fragile; her face showed tired lines. Yet she said with surprising animation, "Why, of course, Cam! I never thought of that."

"Did Dad know any Arabs?" Dutch asked.

Mrs. Schildecker nodded. "Your father made two business trips to Egypt. To buy long-staple Egyptian cotton for Riverlawn Textiles. In fact, it was in Egypt that he contracted his hepatitis. You remember that." Her voice dropped. "I suppose he must have known Arabs in Egypt."

Dutch said, "Did he buy anything besides cotton in Egypt, Mom? Anything valuable that this Arab TV man could have been after?"

"Oh, no, Dutch. I'm sure he didn't. I would have known."

"Wait a minute," Cam said suddenly. "When was Mr. Schildecker in Egypt last, Mrs. Schildecker?"

"Four years ago, Cam. It was his last trip abroad before he died. To Cairo."

Cam turned to Dutch. "Isn't that about when you told me the Tut-ankh-amen collection was robbed in Cairo?"

"Yes, but…" Dutch stood up slowly, clenching his fists.

"I'm sorry," Cam stuttered, realizing all at once the unfortunate implication of his question. In embarrassment he said, "I didn't mean that your Dad could have had anything to do with that."

"Of course you didn't, Cam." Mrs. Schildecker smiled.

"Not Dad," Dutch said fiercely. "He never had a dishonest thought in his life!"

"Forget it," Cam said. "I told you I didn't mean it that way."

"How'd you mean it, then?"

"I meant there could be a possible connection between the Oscar Schildecker name and the fake Arab TV man, that's all. And it could be a connection between you Schildeckers and the stolen Egyptian fingertips at the museum."

"Yeah," Dutch said slowly. "It's possible."

Cam said, "Don't you think we ought to tell Joe Barry about this Arabic paper right away?"

For a long moment Dutch looked at his mother, then turned to his friend. "I don't think I will," he said quietly. "In the first place, Joe already knows my TV man talked kind of funny. And that's the only help toward finding him that Joe'd get out of knowing he was an Arab. Joe doesn't think there's any connection between our TV man and the museum, anyway. And also if we told Joe of this possible connection, it might give him and the police some wrong ideas about my father. Mom and I don't want that."

Cam nodded. "I can see how you feel."

"Besides, I don't want to give Joe any more false leads. This one is even more farfetched than the hunched shoulders thing."

"How about the second address on that scrap of paper?" Cam protested. "That could turn out to be a darn good clue!"

Dutch hesitated. "I don't think Joe could run it down himself," he said then. "Conawachie is a hundred miles away. Out of Joe's territory."

"Jurisdiction," Mrs. Schildecker said. "But Sergeant Barry could ask the Conawachie police to investigate for him."

Dutch said, "Yeah, I suppose so," with a notable lack of enthusiasm.

"You frustrated detective!" Cam laughed suddenly. "You want to run down that Cosgrove clue yourself! Isn't that it? Don't you?"

Sheepishly Dutch nodded. "I sure do."

Cam looked at Dutch's mother with an engaging grin. "Why not?" he asked. "We could drive up to Conawachie, Saturday, say, in my jalopy…"

"Honest, Cam? Would you?" Dutch's face lit up with eagerness.

"Sure." Cam began to embroider on the idea. "We can take Kathy and Janet with us, call on Natalie Cosgrove, get a swim, have a picnic on the beach at Conawachie Inn, and be home in Riverlawn again by ten o'clock Saturday night!" Both boys were familiar with Conawachie. They had visited the town twice with Riverlawn athletic teams to play Conawachie High School.

"Janet works all day on Saturday," Dutch objected half-heartedly. "Why not Sunday?"

Cam shook his head. "Aunt Gunvor, my mother's sister from Norway, is arriving Sunday for a visit with us," he said. "And I have to be there when she arrives, or else. It'll have to be Saturday, or *next* weekend." He suggested, "Maybe Janet can get old Wexler to let her off at noon this Saturday, just for once. That should give us enough time. What do you think?"

"I'll ask her," Dutch said. "And she'll ask Wexler. But we'll go to Conawachie anyway? Whether Janet can go or not?"

"Sure. You and Kathy and me. If Kathy's able to go."

"Swell." Dutch turned to his mother. "All right with you, Mom?"

"If you are very careful, Dutch. I don't want you getting knocked out again, heaven knows! But a hundred miles away, you should be safe enough. And the girls. You wouldn't want to involve them in any danger, remember."

"We'll be okay, Mrs. Schildecker," Cam promised blithely.

"Then if it works out, I'll supply the picnic lunch for you," Mrs. Schildecker said, rising. She went back to the basement to empty the washing machine.

Cam said to Dutch, "What about Dr. Kilty, Dutch? Did you tell your boss about the Arabic translation?"

"Yeah. This afternoon. He thought I ought to show it to Joe Barry because names and addresses in Arabic just don't blow around Riverlawn backyards, usually. But he also agreed to leave it to me whether I told Joe or not. It's *my* name in Arabic on the paper, after all, and Dr. Kilty said it's *my* business, therefore, what

I do about it, more than it is the museum's. I told him I'd think it over."

"But maybe it's your father's name."

"I hadn't thought of that then. Or the possible connection with Egypt. I just said I wanted to follow up the clue myself, if it is a clue." Dutch grinned. "You with me?"

"Sure. I'm mad for this detective stuff, myself. So come Saturday it'll be Schildecker and Osborn back on the trail together!"

"With attractive female assistants—I hope!" said Dutch.

CHAPTER 9

Excursion into Peril

At five minutes to twelve, Saturday noon, Cam's jalopy pulled up in front of the museum. Kathy was riding in the front with Cam; Janet sat in the back seat of the ancient convertible, a scarf around her head. Cam had put down the jalopy's cracked canvas top in deference to the sunny golden day. Janet had been excused from work at Wexler's on condition that she gather a quantity of pine cones in the woods surrounding Lake Conawachie and bring them back to Mrs. Wexler, the gift shop's proprietress, to be decorated for sale at Christmas. All the omens seemed favorable for a pleasant outing. Cam switched off the engine and said, "Come on, let's go in and get Dutch. He'll be finished in three minutes."

Janet shivered. "I hope he'll be all right this time," she said. "The last time we came here to pick him up we found him unconscious, remember?"

"It's broad daylight! ' Cam laughed. "What could happen? Come on."

They entered the museum by the big entrance door and walked back through Egyptian Hall to the narrow corridor that led to Dutch's workroom.

As they trooped in, Dutch was cleaning up—putting the plastic cover on his typewriter, gathering up the reference works he had been studying for his new set of labels on the Ti exhibits.

"Your escort has arrived, my good man," Cam proclaimed, "so let's forget about ancient Egypt and hit the road for Conawachie!"

"I'll be right with you, soon as I put these books away," Dutch said. He looked at Janet and smiled and said, "Hi, Jan. It's great you could get off work today. I'm glad you'll be with us."

"I second the motion," Kathy said, "because my folks wouldn't have let me go without you. But now everything's fine. I can hardly wait to get out in the sun on Conawachie Beach and do something drastic about this pale, filing-clerk complexion I have this summer!"

Cam said, "You got your swim trunks and the picnic stuff, Dutch?"

Dutch shook his head. "I figured to pick them up at home on our way out of town. Hilda still had to pack some of the picnic sandwiches for us this morning. But my house is right on the way. Okay?"

"Sure," said Cam. "So let's get on the ball, shall we? Kathy and Janet and I have our swim suits in the Chevy outside. We're all set."

"I am too." Dutch glanced at the clock on his workroom wall. "Quitting time! High noon!" He whistled a bar or two of a song exuberantly. "We're off in a cloud of dust!" They started for the door.

Janet suddenly uttered an exclamation of dismay. "Oh, Dutch," she said, "I forgot to bring a container to carry my pine cones in! I was going to bring a big shopping bag, but I forgot it." She turned apologetically to Cam. "Could we stop at my house, too, Cam? I'm awfully sorry to be so forgetful. But it won't take more than a minute."

Dutch said, "You can get a bag to hold your pine cones at my house when we stop for my stuff, Jan. How big?"

Janet said, "Pretty big, Dutch. Mrs. Wexler wants a whole lot of cones. A suitcase full, at least."

"I'll call Hilda and tell her to have one ready for us," Dutch proposed. "Then we won't lose any time." He dialed his home on the telephone, and when Hilda answered, he said, "Hilda, this is Dutch. We're coming by in a few minutes for the picnic stuff. Is it ready?" He nodded to Cam, who was clowning by rubbing his stomach and pretending to be half starved. "Fine. And Hilda, will you please do one more thing for us? Get down that old brown suitcase in the attic, will you? Janet needs it to carry pine cones in."

Janet, Kathy, and Cam could hear Hilda's voice over the wire saying, "Pine cones! What's she carrying pine cones for? That's the silliest thing I ever heard of to take on a picnic—"

Dutch cut in, "I'll explain when I see you, Hilda. Okay? But get that suitcase ready for us, will you? We'll be there in five minutes. Thanks. G'by."

When Cam braked the Chevy to a stop in front of Schildecker's house a few minutes later, Hilda was standing on the front porch with a straw picnic hamper flanking her on one side, an old brown leather suitcase on the other.

Dutch leaped out of the jalopy, ran up the walk, seized the hamper and suitcase, one in each hand, and explained rapidly to Hilda why Janet needed the empty suitcase.

Hilda wasn't listening very closely, however; she was too busy feasting admiring eyes on Cam and envious ones on Kathy Johnson, who sat quietly beside him in the Chevy.

Dutch stowed the suitcase in a corner of the jalopy's back seat and put the picnic hamper on the floor, out of the direct sunlight. Then he sat down beside Janet and waved a big-brotherly hand in farewell to Hilda, who called a preoccupied "have a good time" after them while wondering dreamily whether Cam really preferred dark-haired girls, or whether he might not sometime work up a liking for strawberry blondes like her.

She watched the departing car as it passed a parked black sedan fifty yards down the street and then disappeared around the corner onto City Line Road, which became State Route 37 at the outskirts of Riverlawn.

"She's darling, Dutch," Janet commented as she turned back from waving to Hilda. "It was sweet of her to get this suitcase for me." Her gaze was warm behind her spectacles.

Dutch laughed. "She thought you were crazy to take pine cones to a picnic," he said, "until I explained to her what you needed the suitcase for."

Kathy said, "I bet all the boys in the freshman class gather around Hilda every chance they get, don't they, Dutch?"

"She likes boys," Dutch admitted. He grinned at the back of Cam's head and added, "but she seems to like them a little older than freshmen."

"Can't blame her for that," Cam said, driving into a gas station with an air and pulling up before the "regular" pump. "I like girls to be a little older than freshmen, too." He smiled at Kathy and said to the station attendant who came over to the car, "Fill 'er up with regular gas, please."

"You'd do better to buy the premium for this baby," the young attendant said. "No roughness or knocking then. More speed, too."

"Premium?" Cam exploded, insulted. "Why, I personally developed this car's appetite for the cheapest grade of gas there is! She'll run on straight kerosene! And she'll go farther and faster and smoother on regular gas than any other 1941 car can go on premium gas!"

The attendant grinned. "Pardon me," he said, putting the nozzle of the gas hose in the gas tank pipe. "I didn't know this was a specially cut-down, souped-up model, driven only by all-state halfbacks on Saturday afternoons!" He recognized Cam.

"Well, it is," Cam said. "You ought to see this thing go!"

He turned around as a strange voice said in an amused, liquid-smooth tone: "I'd like to see it go, young man. If it's as good as you say, it must be something to see."

The speaker, who had climbed out of a black sedan drawn up to the gasoline pump behind Cam's Chevy, was standing beside the jalopy now, regarding it and its occupants with beaming brown eyes. He was clean-shaven and swarthy; he wore a dark suit, slightly shiny in elbow and knee; a coconut straw hat covered his head so thoroughly that the brim rode on Iris ears; and he had a pair of bushy white eyebrows so rough and shaggy that they almost concealed from view the jolly brown eyes under them. The white eyebrows made him look older than he was.

Cam, who couldn't resist any compliment paid his beloved jalopy, said, "It's a pretty fast job, sir," with a touch of embarrassment that his boasting to the gas station attendant had been overheard. "It'll do eighty or ninety, I bet."

"You ever had it wide open?" the man inquired, his eyes moving critically over the dilapidated convertible.

"No, sir," Cam responded. "But I know what it'll do. I spent all last summer working on it, before I got my driver's license…"

Dutch laughed and said to the man with the white eyebrows, "What he means is, when he bought this wreck, his father made him promise never to drive faster than the speed limit. So he doesn't."

"Very commendable in a young fellow, very. Wish more of our teen-agers followed the same rule of safe driving," the man said. "Bound on a trip?"

Kathy, who had been watching the stranger silently, said, "Just a little picnic outing. We're not going far."

"Where?" asked the man.

"Not far," Kathy said again.

Cam looked at her, puzzled by the unaccustomed coolness in her voice.

Janet interposed hastily, "We all live in Riverlawn. Do you?"

"No, I'm just passing through. Stopped here for gas. I'm from the other end of the state."

The gasoline attendant said to Cam, "That'll be four dollars and five cents."

Cam paid him and started the motor. "You hear that deep purr?" he asked the man proudly.

The stranger grinned. "I hear it," he said. "Have fun." He went back to his own car. "Nice youngsters," he commented to the attendant who was wiping off his windshield.

The attendant shrugged indifferently.

* * * *

The jalopy, under Cam's caressing hands, pointed her nose north on Route 37 and hummed over the smooth concrete surface as lightly as a contented fly skimming a table top.

"There," said Cam, "was a very friendly and discriminating guy. He knows a good car when he sees one."

"Friendly and discriminating," Janet said slowly, "aren't exactly the words I'd apply to him."

"I wouldn't either," Kathy seconded her.

"I thought you sounded a mite snippy to him," Cam observed lazily. "What would be the word you'd apply to old White Eyebrows, then?"

Without hesitation, Janet answered, "Nosy."

"Nosy?" Dutch chuckled. "Why, Janet! The guy was just trying to be a pal. A little curious, maybe…"

"Not curious," Kathy said. "'Nosy' is exactly the right word. Asking us where we were going! Really! It was none of his business, a perfect stranger like that! And looking at us and everything in the car as though we were criminals with a carload of stolen loot!"

Cam said, "My, my! Dutch, did *you* notice this guy's nosiness?"

"Not me," said Dutch, bending his head back to look at the fleecy clouds that floated above them. "But then, men aren't as sensitive as girls, Cam. Personally, all I noticed about the guy was that his suit was kind of shiny and he had shaggy white eyebrows. And also that he was driving a black Plymouth sedan. Rented."

Cam glanced into his rear-view mirror at Dutch in surprise. "Rented?"

"Yeah. The rental company's insignia was on the front grille."

"Anyway," Kathy said as though it ended the discussion, "I'm glad I froze him."

"B-r-r-r!" Cam pretended to shiver. "I hope you never use that cool, cool voice on me, Kathy! You sounded like Mrs. Astor addressing the milkman's horse!"

Kathy laughed. "I wasn't that bad," she protested.

"Listen," Dutch said, "if Cam's jalopy can fly, as he claimed to that man back there, we'll be at Conawachie before we know it. What's the plan for the afternoon?"

Janet said, "We go swimming at Conawachie Beach; we gather pine cones for Mrs. Wexler; we have our picnic on the beach."

"Sure," Cam agreed. "What's wrong with that?"

"Nothing," Dutch said. "But how about Mrs. or Miss Cosgrove?" He and Cam had told the girls about the clue of the scrap of paper with the two names and addresses written on it in Arabic.

"As soon as we get there," Cam said, "let's get that off our minds first."

"Can't we come with you to interview her?" Janet asked wistfully. "I have a feeling she'll tell you something important."

Dutch shook his head. "I'm sorry, Jan. You two stay at Conawachie Beach or gather pine cones while Cam and I go find the Cosgrove gal. I promised Mother we wouldn't let you get mixed up in this thing any further."

Janet didn't insist. She merely nodded and laughed and said, "Well, as a matter of fact, I never expected I'd be this close to a real detective, not to mention participating in a case!" She looked at Dutch sitting beside her and patted his hand. "So Kathy and I will wait for you two sleuths in our bower by the sea."

"By the lake," Cam said.

"And what exactly is a bower?" Dutch asked.

"What do you care," Kathy returned, "as long as we'll be in it?"

"Don't press your luck, Dutch," Cam said. He looked into the side mirror that gave him a view of the road behind them. "Here comes your nosy friend from the service station, girls."

Dutch and the girls turned their heads. A black Plymouth sedan was traveling several hundred yards behind.

"It can't be the same car," Janet announced at once. "There are two people in it. White Eyebrows was traveling alone, I thought."

"He was."

"Well, I can see two in the front seat of this car back of us."

"It's a different car, then."

"Maybe," Dutch cut in. "But it has the same rental insignia on the grille."

"Coincidence is the thief of time," Kathy misquoted solemnly.

Cam laughed. "If it is the same man," he said to Kathy, "it's your fault he's following us. You wouldn't tell him where we were going. So he decided to see for himself."

"Oh!" For a moment Kathy thought Cam was serious. Then she realized he was teasing her. "I honestly didn't like that little man, all the same," she maintained stoutly. "For a perfect stranger, he was too interested in us and our car."

"You're giving me goosebumps, Kathy!" Janet said. "Do you mean you think he was interested in us in a sinister way?"

"I don't know. I just had this feeling about him."

"Well," Cam reassured them, "you can breathe easier soon. In another half mile we turn off this road onto Route Seventy-one for Conawachie, Indian Bluff, and Sackening. And our friend back there will probably stick right on this road and go on about his innocent business, whatever it is."

"Good!" Janet said, relieved. "I didn't like him, either, to tell the truth. And it wasn't just because girls are more sensitive than boys, Dutch!"

"More likely because you're more beautiful than we are," Cam offered.

"Sure," said Dutch. "Show me a guy who wouldn't be interested in you two gorgeous things, and I'll show you a guy who has lost all interest in life, who has a long gray beard…"

"And white eyebrows," finished Janet, laughing.

Cam slowed and took the turn from the broad, straight concrete highway into the narrower, winding black-top road that was Route 71. When they looked back from the first twist of the new road and failed to see the black Plymouth behind them, they began to chat gaily about shaking off their pursuer.

Their good spirits lasted only a few miles, however. For then Dutch looked back once more and said quietly, "He's with us again."

The girls swung around in their seats and both spotted the black car before another bend in the road hid it.

"Dutch," said Janet then, very seriously, "I think that car is following us. It isn't just imagination. They stay the same distance behind us…"

"Simmer down, kids," Cam interrupted calmly. "It's nothing to worry about, Janet. I could leave that car of theirs behind like a turtle with a sore toe if I wanted to.

Kathy moved a little closer to Cam and said in a worried voice, "Well, why don't you want to? Let's!"

Dutch scanned the road ahead as far as he could see. There was no sign of another car. And behind them the black Plymouth was the only car they had seen for a full five minutes. Traffic on Route 71 had been exceptionally light. This road, thought Dutch, was not only a narrow, twisting one, but a lonely one, too.

The faint beginnings of uneasiness stirred in him—little dust devils of worry that refused to be put down. "Cam," he said, turning to look behind them once again, "I think maybe Kathy has a point. If you can outrun this car behind us…"

Then he stopped speaking suddenly. For the black sedan that pursued them was no longer hanging back several hundred yards. It was almost upon them, turning out to pass as a long straight stretch of road appeared before them.

It gained on them rapidly. Dutch could make out now the patches of white eyebrow that unmistakably identified the driver as their recent acquaintance. He was conscious of the other man in the black car, too, but only in a vague way. His attention was centered on the driver.

As the grille of the Plymouth began to draw even with the jalopy's rear fender, Dutch thought: He's just another motorist, in a bigger hurry than we are, that's all. If he was interested in us, he wouldn't be passing us. He'd still be following us. He just happens to be going our way. It's perfectly natural. He's a normal, ordinary-type guy. He'll probably give us a toot on his horn and wave to us when he sees we're the kids he spoke to in the gas station back in Riverlawn. What am I getting all excited about? That museum mystery must be working on my nerves.

These thoughts, skittering through his head like a flock of wind-driven sparrows in a spring storm, settled to rest with a swoop when Cam said, "Hey! What do you know? Old White Eyebrows there wants a drag race!

"Now, Cam!" Kathy warned.

"I won't give him one," Cam promised regretfully. "But he said he'd like to see this old baby really go, didn't he? Back there in the gas station?"

Of course, Dutch thought with relief. That's it. He recognized us and wants to see whether Cam's car will really go as fast as Cam said it would.

"I wish I could let her out a few notches," muttered Cam disconsolately. "I'd show him how to fly!" But as the black Plymouth drew up abreast of him Cam touched his brake to make it easier for the black car to pass.

"Let them get ahead of us," Janet urged. "Then we won't have to worry about them anymore."

"Yeah," said Dutch. He looked more closely at the man who sat beside White Eyebrows. Was he a hitchhiker? Somebody White Eyebrows had picked up on the road since leaving Riverlawn? He seemed to be taller than the driver. At least he sat higher in the seat. He was hatless, with a black crewcut. He wore a faded sports shirt striped in blue and green. And he kept Iris eyes studiously front, not turning to look at the car his companion was passing.

That's kind of funny, Dutch thought. He took another look at the hitchhiker, and his throat closed up suddenly, so that he had difficulty in forcing out the words to Cam, "Let them pass, Cam. Let them pass."

"I'm trying to," Cam returned, slowing down still more, "but the crazy guy won't go by." The two cars, neck and neck now, rolled at forty miles an hour down the long straight stretch of Route 71, bouncing over the rough asphalt surface.

"You're racing him, Cam Osborn!" Kathy said indignantly.

"I'm not, Kathy. Can't you see I'm trying to let him pass?"

"Then why doesn't he?" Janet asked. She took a tight grip with both hands on Dutch's arm. "Why doesn't he?"

Dutch looked at the jaunty face of the white-eyebrowed driver in the other car, and said, "He's grinning. He's enjoying this, Cam."

"I'm not," said Cam. "He's trying to force us off the road, Dutch."

It was true. The black Plymouth was edging farther and farther to the right, closer and closer to Cam's jalopy. To keep clear of it, Cam was driving closer and closer to the right-hand edge of the road which here consisted of nothing but a weed-grown ditch.

Kathy gasped. Janet squeezed Dutch's arm more tightly. And Dutch, who had been aware of the black sedan's maneuver before Cam voiced it, merely said in a strained voice, "That's right, Cam. But don't let him."

Cam, whose sporting blood had been aroused by his earlier conviction that the black car wanted to race him, now realized that he was facing something more serious than a challenge to a friendly road race. Immediately the cool precise assessment of conditions that had helped to make him a star halfback at Riverlawn High asserted itself. His accurate judgment of distance, his split-second timing, the instantaneous response of his muscles automatically made him do the right thing in the tight situation that confronted him now.

In a carefree voice that did much to calm Kathy and Janet, he said, "Who do they think they are? They can't do this to us! Hold tight, kids!"

With these words he increased the jalopy's speed suddenly, gradually pulling farther to the right until his wheels were skimming the edge of the roadside ditch. The black sedan speeded up to stay even with the Chevy, inching farther and farther to the right in its turn, obviously intent on preventing Cam from escaping the trap closing upon him. There was no doubt of it now: White Eyebrows wanted to force Cam into the ditch.

For thirty seconds, while both cars gained speed, Cam let him think he would succeed. Then, at the last possible second, he hit his footbrake with violent suddenness, throwing his gear lever into neutral simultaneously so the jalopy wouldn't stall. The old car almost stood on its nose. It came to a sliding screeching near-stop, and the smell of scorched rubber filled their nostrils.

The black sedan, still inching to the right, shot ahead of them, confident that Cam's car had actually gone into the ditch; it pulled clear over to the road's right edge, slowing abruptly.

But Cam's jalopy paused only momentarily. He twitched into second gear, twisted his wheel to the left, and fed gas at the same moment. A deep powerful roar under the battered hood rewarded him. The old car leaped forward like a grayhound in need of exercise.

As he accelerated, Cam nonchalantly guided the jalopy to the left of the Plymouth, shifting into high gear and swishing by on the left side, his hand raised in a mocking wave to White Eyebrows. The black sedan immediately put on speed. Twisting to look back, Dutch could see it make an obvious effort to catch the jalopy. But now the road became a series of dangerous curves again; and Cam drove his souped-up car at such a gait that the black car was soon lost to view behind them, falling farther and farther behind in a hopeless chase.

"I hope my father'll understand why I'm breaking my promise to him about speeding," Cam said, laughing at Kathy's tense expression. "That guy wasn't fooling, was he? But he can't catch us now, so relax, everybody."

Dutch released a long-held breath, putting up his hand to touch Janet's, which was still clasped around his arm. "That was close," he said solemnly. "And it was deliberate, Cam. I'm glad you got us out of that mess, because I think I recognized the second man in the car."

"Recognized him?" Janet let go of Dutch's arm and adjusted her glasses with a hand that trembled slightly. "Who was it?"

Cam was feeling the reaction of relief, now that he had left the black sedan far behind. He said with an infectious chuckle, "Don't tell us, Dutch. Let us guess."

"All right, guess," Kathy urged him. "Who was it?"

Cam caught Dutch's eye in the rear view mirror. "Hunched shoulders?" he asked, grinning. "Right?"

"Right." Dutch nodded positively. "The guy had black crewcut hair instead of being half bald, but I'd swear he was the man who tried to rob my house and knocked me out in the museum!"

CHAPTER 10

A Clue at Conawachie

At twenty minutes to two Cam pulled up in the parking lot at Conawachie Inn.

The inn, a rambling rustic hostelry built of peeled and varnished logs, was set on the wooded south shore of Lake Conawachie. Shining white sea sand had been imported at considerable expense to build a beach before the inn. Fortunately it wasn't necessary to be a paying guest to utilize this beach; the inn collected a nominal fee from bathers for dressing room privileges.

Dutch and Cam paid the two dollars for two dressing rooms. The girls disappeared at once to change, but Cam and Dutch decided not to change to swim suits until after talking with Natalie Cosgrove.

While the girls were gone Dutch retrieved the picnic hamper from the car and carried it, along with the empty suitcase intended to contain Janet's pine cones, to a spot on the beach as distant as possible from the inn entrance. Here the beach was comparatively free of bathers. And here, too, the towering pines of the virgin forest surrounding the lake crowded close to the beach—a promising source of fallen pine cones for Janet.

Cam followed Dutch, bearing a portable radio, a beach blanket, and four candy bars. The boys sat down on the blanket and waited for the girls to appear from the dressing rooms up the beach.

"How about that black Plymouth?" Cam said, his false cheerfulness vanished now. "That could have been serious, Dutch."

Dutch nodded. "Play it down to the girls, Cam. Okay? I shouldn't have mentioned that I recognized the tall man, but I was rattled. It frightened Janet and Kathy pretty badly, I'm afraid."

"They've got nothing on me!" Cam said. "I'm scared stiff myself. What's that pair of monkeys got against us? Or you, rather? They really tried to pile us up."

"I know it. But I don't know why. It doesn't make sense, any more than breaking into my house or robbing the museum makes sense. You think they can find us here?"

Cam looked around them at the crowded beach. "Too many people for them to try anything here, even if they do find us. Besides, that road we left them on can take them to Indian Bluff or Sackening as well as here. Let's hope they try to find us in Indian Bluff or Sackening before they try Conawachie. White Eyebrows couldn't have known where we were going." Dutch grinned. "That's right. Kathy and Janet sure wouldn't tell him, would they?"

"You know something? Those two girls are smarter than we are, Dutch. They said they thought White Eyebrows was too interested in us."

"But we knew better. How dumb can you be?" Dutch waved to Janet and Kathy, who had appeared on the beach. "Let's forget it for a while, shall we? You think the girls will be safe here while we're interviewing Natalie Cosgrove?"

"Sure. Look at all the people on the beach."

"I guess you're right." Dutch tried to hide his uneasiness.

Janet and Kathy reached them then, very sleek and lovely in their bathing suits and slightly flushed with self-consciousness as the boys whistled admiringly. They dropped onto the blanket and groped in their beach bags for suntan lotion.

"There," said Janet. "Now we're settled, Dutch. You and Cam can go and find your mystery woman. Kathy and I will be perfectly all right here. But hurry back." Her voice still held the memory of their recent fright.

"We shouldn't be gone long," Dutch replied. "There's your suitcase for the pine cones, Jan. You ought to find plenty right there in the woods by the beach." He pointed.

Cam said, "Wait'll we come back before you go in swimming, will you? We don't want any local boys muscling in on us."

"We'll wait." Kathy laughed. "Don't worry. Swimming is the only sport I can beat you at, Cam, and I aim to prove it to you today." Then she sobered. "I hope Natalie What's-her-name can tell you something helpful, Dutch. Although I think this whole thing has gotten too serious now for you boys to try to solve it all by yourselves. Don't you, Janet?"

Janet nodded a vigorous agreement.

Dutch forced a light-hearted shrug. "Could be. But I'm not going to let it spoil the day for us—or you. Have fun, kids. We'll be back in a flash."

* * * *

"What was that address again?" Cam asked as they drove slowly out of the inn parking lot onto Lake Drive. Lake Drive completely encircled Lake Conawachie and gave access to its cottages, fishing camps, and motor lodges.

"I'll never forget it," Dutch said. "Natalie R. Cosgrove, Lake Drive, Conawachie, New York."

"No street number."

"No. A number would have tipped off that they were addresses, even in Arabic. There wasn't any street number for my house, either."

"What'll we do then?"

"Looking in a phone book's probably our best bet. Stop at this drug store, huh?"

Dutch went into the drug store that occupied one corner of the Conawachie village crossroads. When he came out, he nodded to Cam and said, "Seven-twenty-six Lake Drive. That's the road we're on. And Seven-twenty-six is north."

Without a word Cam put the jalopy in gear and drove slowly northward on Lake Drive. Both boys kept a weather eye out for any sign of the black Plymouth. Within half a mile, they came to a cluster of homes between the road and the lake shore, and Dutch found the number 726 on a neat, white clapboard house with a screened-in porch that nestled attractively under two big pine trees.

"There it is, Cam…that house there."

"Swell." Cam pulled up immediately, parking his car at the edge of the road two houses away, the only parking spot that offered. "Looks like an all-year-round house, doesn't it? Not just a summer cottage."

"Gee, I hope somebody's home!" said Dutch suddenly. "I never thought of that!"

"Neither did I. But maybe our luck's in. I think I see a lady sitting on that screened porch." They stepped out of the car onto a soft mat of pine needles and walked along the road edge toward 726.

When Dutch pulled open the screen door to the porch and said hesitantly, "Is this the Cosgrove house?" the middle-aged woman sitting inside on a plastic chaise gave him a pleasant smile and said, "That's right. Won't you come in?"

"Thanks." The boys stood awkwardly inside the screen door, not sure how to proceed. "Is it *Mrs.* Cosgrove?" Dutch ventured after a pause.

"Yes. I'm Mrs. Cosgrove. Can I help you?"

Dutch blurted, "Mrs. Cosgrove, we don't know, to tell you the truth. But we hope so. I'm Dutch Schildecker and this is my friend, Cam Osborn. We live in Riverlawn and we came to see you because we found your address written in Arabic on a scrap of paper we found under my back hedge."

Mrs. Cosgrove's wide-set hazel eyes stared at Dutch as though he were mentally afflicted. She put up a hand to her graying hair. "How was that again?" she asked, bewildered. "My address in *Arabic?*"

Cam laughed uneasily. "We're not absolutely crazy, Mrs. Cosgrove, even if we do sound that way. Dutch means that we're mixed up in some very peculiar happenings in Riverlawn, and we hope you'll be able to help us find an answer to them." Cam thought that sounded quite professional. He spread his hands in a spontaneous gesture, asking for understanding.

Mrs. Cosgrove tried unsuccessfully to hide a smile. "I see," she said then. "Why don't you sit down, boys, and tell me about it?"

"Thank you." Dutch and Cam sat down stiffly in two woven plastic chairs facing Mrs. Cosgrove.

She said, "Did you come all the way from Riverlawn to Conawachie just to see me?"

"If your name is Natalie R. Cosgrove, we did," Dutch said with unintentional bluntness.

"It is. My husband is the principal of Conawachie High School. Right now he's out there on the lake, fishing." She waved a hand toward the lake and smiled again.

Her manner put the boys at ease. She seemed pleasant, interested, and quite willing to listen to their story. So Dutch, acting as spokesman, plunged into an account of his adventures at once. He showed her the original scrap of paper which he had brought with him, and the translation sheet prepared by Mr. Petri of the Bertrand Language School. And finally, he told her about what had happened on Route 71 when the black sedan had attempted to force them off the road just an hour ago.

Mrs. Cosgrove listened raptly, watching Dutch's earnest expressive face and biting her upper lip at the more dramatic points of the recital. From time to time she glanced at Cam as though for confirmation of this strange tale, and each time Cam nodded his head at her vigorously.

"Goodness!" she exclaimed, when Dutch paused for breath. "You do have a mystery to solve, don't you? A dangerous one, too, apparently. I should think you'd call on the Riverlawn police to help you."

"We have, Mrs. Cosgrove." This was Cam. "But they're as much in the dark as we are."

"We hoped you might be able to think of some reason why your name should appear on that paper in Arabic," Dutch urged.

She was silent, thinking. At length she shook her head. "I'm afraid not, Dutch." She used his first name naturally, expressing her sympathy for his disappointment. "It's as puzzling to me as it is to you. Although"—she sat up with a jerk in the chaise—"you did say it was a set of ancient Egyptian fingertips that were stolen from your museum?"

"Yes, Ma'am," Dutch affirmed.

Mrs. Cosgrove said, "That's the only possible connection with me that I can see. And it's very tenuous." She leaned back again.

"Any connection would help," Dutch said.

"Well, I've been to Egypt, that's all. And there are lots of Arabs in Egypt. So the Arabic writing and the Egyptian antiquities…"

Dutch grew excited. "You've been to Egypt! When was that?"

Mrs. Cosgrove thought. "Why, my husband and I took a Mediterranean cruise during his last sabbatical. That would have been four years ago. We stopped at Alexandria and took a side trip to Cairo for three days."

"If that's my father's name on the scrap of paper and not mine," Dutch said, "it might mean something. Because my father had been to Egypt, too. Four years ago. The same year as you and your husband."

"Yeah, but what would it mean?" Cam rubbed his blond head. "Just a trip to Egypt." He paused, then asked, "Did you happen to visit the National Museum in Cairo, where the genuine Tut-ankh-amen fingertips were stolen from?"

Mrs. Cosgrove nodded. "Of course. Every American tourist who goes to Cairo goes to see those relics. But I don't remember any gold fingernail covers."

"Still, there might be a connection," Cam said.

"No, Cam," Dutch contradicted. "Because my father didn't go to visit the National Museum. He was in Cairo strictly on business, buying cotton, Mom says."

Mrs. Cosgrove was quiet for a time. Dutch and Cam waited. When she spoke, it wasn't much help. She said, "We do have that one interesting fact, anyway, for you to tell your Riverlawn police about, Dutch: that both your father and I visited Cairo the same year, and both his name and mine appear in Arabic on your scrap of paper."

"Maybe Joe Barry can make something of that, ' said Dutch to Cam, "but I sure can't. Can you?"

"Nope." Cam grinned disarmingly at Mrs. Cosgrove and tapped his head. "Dutch depends on me for his deductive work," he explained. "He thinks I have a very unusual mentality."

"I'm sure you have." Mrs. Cosgrove returned his smile. "I wish I could give you some more helpful information."

"That was just a gag," Dutch said. "Cam's as much in the dark as I am. But thanks for trying to help us, and we'll certainly let you know if we figure out anything about this, or if the police do. Because you're mixed up in it, too, whatever it is, Mrs. Cosgrove."

"I suppose I am," she said.

Dutch had been staring through the side screen of the porch to-ward the lake. On impulse, and without much hope of uncovering anything further from Mrs. Cosgrove, he turned back to her and asked, "I don't suppose any TV repairmen or telephone linemen or anybody like that's been hanging around your house lately, have they? Trying to come into your house and fix something that's not broken?"

She shook her head. "Not a single one, Dutch," she laughed. "And I'm truly sorry for your sake. This is a very small community, remember. My husband and I know almost everybody in it, even the regular summer visitors. So I'd have certainly known it if any strangers were interested in my house."

"These are pretty smooth operators," Dutch said. "And they keep out of sight. But I was afraid you'd say that. Since the Arabs tried to break into my house, I thought there was a bare chance they might have tried to burgle yours, too."

"Burgle!" Mrs. Cosgrove sat up straight again, evidently electrified by a new thought. "Maybe that was it!"

Dutch felt the hairs on the back of his neck rise. "What?" he asked.

"Maybe somebody stole that car case I couldn't find." Mrs. Cosgrove's expression became reminiscent. "On Monday I looked everywhere for an old car case—you know, one of those dress holders that folds up. I planned to pack my dresses in it when my husband and I go off tomorrow for a week's auto trip to Virginia. I couldn't find a trace of it, although I was certain I saw it in its usual place in the storage room not long ago."

Cam said, "You haven't found it yet?"

"No. I bought a new one yesterday to replace it."

Dutch said, "You didn't notice any signs that somebody may have broken into your house, did you?"

"No, Dutch. Until this minute I thought I'd merely thrown the bag away and didn't remember, or had absent-mindedly given it to our church rummage sale, or something of the sort."

Cam said, "I bet it was stolen!"

"It figures," Dutch said quietly. "And if so, we have another fact, another odd set of coincidences, at least: your house was robbed recently, my house was recently attempted, and the River-lawn Museum was robbed recently. And all three events more or less connected by that Arabic writing on the scrap of paper."

"Wait'll we tell Joe Barry that!" Cam cried. "That's something he can really get his teeth into Dutch. Especially if…"

"Wait!" Dutch held up his hand to stop Cam's words. "Let's ask Mrs. Cosgrove before we jump to any conclusions, Cam." He turned to the principal's wife. "Mrs. Cosgrove, was your car case, this one that may have been stolen, part of the luggage you took to Egypt on your Mediterranean cruise four years ago? You said it was an old case."

They waited anxiously for her reply. "Yes," she said at length, "I took it on the cruise, I know, and I think I remember taking it with us when we left the ship at Alexandria for our side trip to Cairo."

"Thanks a million," Dutch said. "You've helped us a lot, Mrs. Cosgrove." He stood up and Cam followed suit. "We'll turn this information over to the Riverlawn police right away. And we'll let you know what develops."

Mrs. Cosgrove arose, too. "Please do," she said with a smile. "My curiosity will kill me if you don't. I hope you solve our mystery very soon. Shall I call in our Conawachie police and tell them about it, too?"

"Not right away, if you don't mind," Dutch said. "We might alarm the Arabs and lose this chance. But if Sergeant Barry of our police should want to get in touch with you…"

"My telephone number is Conawachie 71318. Tell him I'll do anything I can to help."

"Thanks ever so much," Dutch said.

They went out, closing the screen door quietly behind them.

Once outside, with the sharp clean tang of the pine woods in their nostrils, Cam and Dutch hurried toward Cam's jalopy, parked fifty yards down the road from Mrs. Cosgrove's house.

They were both so excited about what they had learned from the principal's wife that at first their conversation was no more than a series of interruptions, as each eagerly attempted to interpret this fresh information to the other. Preoccupied as they were with speculations, it wasn't until they were almost upon Cam's car that they noticed its engine hood was raised and a man in a shiny-seated suit was bending over examining its motor so carefully that his head and shoulders were almost hidden under the lifted hood.

"Hey!" said Cam indignantly. "Look at that!"

"Some nerve!" Dutch said. "A snooper!"

They ran the last few steps to the car. "Excuse me," said Cam, taking the man by the shoulder none too gently. "That's my car you're messing with, Mister. Out!" He pulled strongly on the man's shoulder, yanked him away from the engine, and turned him around against the car's front fender. "What's the idea?" Cam asked angrily.

Then his mouth opened with surprise.

The shaggy white eyebrows were missing. The too-big coconut straw hat riding on the ears was gone, too, revealing close-cut black hair. But the skin was still dark and swarthy; the brown eyes were still beaming and jolly; and the voice was still liquid smooth when the man said softly, "Let's not get rough, boys, all right? I'm just taking a look at your power plant."

"Why, you!" Cam said in a tight, dangerous voice. "You're the guy that nearly ditched us a little while ago! Only then you had white eyebrows. Didn't he, Dutch?"

Dutch didn't get a chance to answer.

Another voice, which he instantly recognized by its hoarseness and the faint flavor of a foreign accent, spoke from above their heads.

"Hold it, kids!" the voice said. "Before somebody gets hurt."

Cam jerked around. Dutch glanced at the jalopy and saw that the tall, hunch-shouldered TV man, so recently a passenger in White Eyebrow's sedan, had risen from concealment under the dashboard of Cam's car and was leaning negligently on the top frame of the windshield.

In one big hand he held an ugly, short-barreled revolver, pointed directly at Cam's head.

CHAPTER 11

The Shed in the Woods

For an instant Dutch felt nothing but shock. He looked at the tall hunched figure regarding him over the windshield of Cam's car. The small gun, almost hidden in the man's hand, peeped at them with metallic menace. The black eye of its short barrel, peering steadily at Cam, looked as big as the mouth of a cave to Dutch. And he had no shadow of doubt, all at once, that if Cam should fail to do exactly what these men ordered him to, that midget revolver would cough death toward Cam at such a speed that not even an all-state halfback could dodge it.

Dutch's sense of shock gave way to fear. For he suddenly realized what a dangerous business he and Cam had unwittingly become involved in. These two men were more than petty burglars, more than minor lawbreakers, more than good-natured light-opera crooks with prop blackjacks up their sleeves to use reluctantly on museum employees. These were men who would stop at nothing to achieve their ends.

Dutch saw the highway incident in true perspective now: a deliberate attempt to force four inoffensive youngsters off the road by men callously indifferent to any injury or death that might result. These were big-league operators, Dutch confessed to himself—far too dangerous for a couple of seventeen-year-old amateur detectives to take on. What had he and Cam been thinking of, not to tell Joe Barry every thing they had learned about that scrap of paper? This was a job for pros to handle, not two high school boys!

But it was too late for regrets; just looking at that gun pointed at Cam's head scared Dutch half to death. For Cam was courageous. He had a fiery temper when aroused. He was also unpredictable.

Dutch was not certain that even a leveled revolver would keep Cam from expressing himself violently in a situation like this.

These thoughts raced through Dutch's mind while the tall man's words still hung in the piney air. Those words had frozen the whole scene into motionlessness, as a high-speed camera freezes action in mid-movement. Cam still had his hand on White Eyebrow's shoulder, still was staring incredulously at the man with the gun. Dutch himself was standing slightly crooked on one foot, tilted by a fallen pine cone under his shoe, his eyes on the TV man.

With an effort he tore his eyes away and saw that, as he feared, Cam was making a lightning recovery from his surprise and was rapidly generating enough anger to launch him into reckless action at any moment.

Dutch put out a hand, clamped it on his friend's wrist, and said as steadily as he could, "Easy, pal. Take it easy. The man's serious. We don't want to get shot."

"Aren't you the sensible one?" the short man said to Dutch with a laugh. He sneered at Cam. "That's good advice, Muscles. Take it." He knocked Cam's hand from his shoulder. Cam permitted him to do so, now fully awake to their danger.

"This is very nice," the tall man said conversationally over his gun, "but a trifle public to hold a private meeting." He looked up and down the road. Nobody was in sight. And even if there were, Dutch thought, there was nothing about this informal group around a battered jalopy to draw undue attention. The cottage before which they stood was shuttered and empty. But surely on this lakeside road it could not be long before someone came along? Dutch prayed fervently that somebody would—preferably a squad of U.S. Marines, fully armed.

With a smooth movement that did not disturb the aim of his gun in the slightest, the tall man jumped down from the jalopy and said in a neutral voice, "Let's move down this way, boys, to where our car is parked. Then we'll all be more comfortable."

Without a word Dutch and Cam turned and walked after the shorter man while the tall gun-bearer shepherded them along from the rear. The black sedan with the rental insignia on its grille stood under a tree beside the road, a hundred yards away. It was facing south, toward the village.

Urged by the gun at their backs, Cam and Dutch climbed into the front seat beside White Eyebrows. The tall man with the gun got in back, explaining sardonically that from there he would be able to hit anything he shot at without any possible chance of missing.

Cam looked sidelong at Dutch and shrugged slightly. Cam got the message, Dutch thought with enormous relief. He won't try anything. Maybe he's scared, too, now that he sees how tough these fellows really are.

He was partially correct. Cam was frightened, all right. What boy in his right mind wouldn't be? Cam was trying to see some way out of this trap in which he and Dutch had so foolishly landed themselves. He knew with certainty that he could take White Eyebrows any time he chose to and not even breathe hard doing it. Provided, of course, that White Eyebrows didn't have a gun tucked away somewhere. His hands on the steering wheel looked weak and characterless, except for the thumbnail on the left hand, which was deformed by an injury and bitten to the quick. But the tall TV man in the back seat was a different proposition altogether. There was dynamite in him, and not just the dynamite he carried in his little revolver, either. Instinct told Cam that the tall man was the more dangerous of the two. And since the gunman had the advantage now, nothing could be gained, Cam thought, by trying to escape from the car himself or diverting the attention of the thieves while Dutch escaped. Just be patient, he told himself. Wait. Maybe a better chance will come later.

With this settled Cam leaned back and relaxed while White Eyebrows started the Plymouth's engine, snapped off the parking brake, and started north on Lake Drive.

They passed Mrs. Cosgrove's house a moment later. Dutch looked desperately for any sign that she might see them go by and sense their danger; but the porch chaise behind the screening was empty now. The house seemed deserted.

"Where are you taking us?" he asked.

The man in the back seat answered him. "Not very far. We need privacy." There was a very sinister ring to the word "privacy" the way he said it.

"What do we need privacy for?" Cam asked boldly. "Can't we talk right here?"

"If you'd rather," the short man said in a tone totally at odds with the jollity of his beaming brown eyes.

"Why not?" Cam said. "Then you won't have a kidnapping charge against you, too."

The man in the back seat said without heat, "Smart kid," and pushed the revolver snout into Cam's neck with cruel force. Cam bent forward to escape it, and Dutch held his breath, terrified lest the tall man pull the trigger.

The driver chuckled. "Heroes," he said. "They're both heroes, these kids. They want you to shoot them, Sal. So why not oblige them?"

The man in the back seat said a single vicious word in a language neither Dutch nor Cam understood. Then he said, "I'm going to explain it to you so you'll know the score. We only want one thing from you. And if you're smart, you'll be anxious to tell it to us. But after you tell it, we'll need a little time to see if you've told us right, and if so, to do what's necessary and be on our way. So right now we're going someplace where we can keep you kids on ice for a little while. Get it?"

Dutch got it. So did Cam. And it didn't do anything to improve their spirits or lessen their fear.

Cam protested, "What do you want to know? Ask us now. We'll promise not to interfere with you afterward."

White Eyebrows laughed again. "Promises. You hear that, Sal?"

The man called Sal didn't laugh. Apparently he never laughed. He sat in silence, letting his menacing presence behind them increase the boys' nervousness.

The sedan reached the northernmost point of the segment of Lake Drive that bordered the eastern margin of the lake. Here, where Lake Drive bent sharply left to continue its encirclement of Lake Conawachie, another road joined it from the east. This was a narrow, unused-looking track, once surfaced with gravel and tar but now fallen into serious disrepair. Its surface was pocked with potholes and ruts. When White Eyebrows turned the Plymouth into it, springs groaned, axles complained, tires thudded, and their progress became a series of jolting bumps. White Eyebrows was forced to slow almost to a walking pace.

Looking ahead through the windshield, Cam and Dutch could see that this lonely road plunged directly through the woods. It ran straight eastward for a few rods, then angled sharply southeast. Where were they being taken?

At length, pressured into speech by the tall man's calculated silence, Dutch asked, "How'd you find us?"

Sal said nothing. But White Eyebrows, who seemed in excellent humor, replied, "We had an idea you were heading for Conawachie when you outran us back there. There's only one road around the lake. So we just drove along Lake Drive until we found your crummy car parked back there where we picked you up."

"Or," said Dutch, "did you think we might be at that particular house? Because you'd been there before yourselves?"

"What's that supposed to mean?" Sal grunted from the back seat in his hoarse voice. He poked the revolver warningly into Dutch's neck this time. It hurt. Dutch bent his head forward instinctively; an icy chill touched his shoulder blades. He managed to say weakly, "Well, you seem to know about Lake Conawachie… and this road…and…"

"Yeah, we do." Sal settled back. "And I've changed my mind. I want to know two things from you now, instead of just one. Glad you reminded me, kid."

"What do you want to know?" Dutch said.

"First, why you went straight to that particular house on Lake Drive, and why you think we've been there before."

Cam said, "Tell him, Dutch. What harm can it do now?"

After a moment's hesitation during which he realized that Cam was right in urging frankness at this point, Dutch said over his shoulder, "I thought you were trying to break into my house in Riverlawn that day you pretended to be a TV man. And I thought I recognized you as the guy who knocked me out in the museum. I wanted to find out what for. And I came across a piece of paper in my backyard that you dropped off your ladder that day at my house. It had addresses on it."

"So that's where it went," Sal said.

With these five words he made tacit admission that he had been the fake TV man and the blackjack artist at the museum, just as Dutch had suspected. But, thought Dutch wryly, so what? What good does it do us to know that now? He felt Cam's elbow nudge his side. That meant Cam recognized Sal's admission of guilt, too. Somehow Dutch felt his courage oozing back into him slowly, re-awakened by that nudge from his friend.

"You could read the addresses?" White Eyebrows asked, amazed.

"No. I got the Language School to translate them for me."

Sal's next words came slowly. "And took them to the River-lawn police, I suppose, like the smart kid you are?"

"No, I didn't. I wasn't sure they meant anything."

White Eyebrows wasn't laughing now. "The kid's lying, Sal," he said anxiously. "And if he is, the cops could be on us any minute."

Sal leaned forward, resting the revolver barrel gently against the back of Dutch's head. "How about that, kid? You lying?"

"Lay off him," Cam said angrily. He took a chance that nothing serious would happen to them until Sal and White Eyebrows had obtained from them whatever information it was they wanted so badly. He put up a hand and boldly pushed the revolver aside from Dutch's head. "Why would he lie to you? He didn't have to tell you about finding the paper in the first place."

"And," added Dutch in a slightly unsteady voice, "if I'd told the cops, they'd be here today instead of us."

Sal leaned back in his seat again. The boys could hear the cushions creak as he shifted his weight. "Yeah," he muttered. "Maybe." But he seemed satisfied. Dutch and Cam released silent sighs of relief.

"We're almost there," White Eyebrows said, "so it don't make much difference anyway."

"Where?" asked Cam.

"Shut up," White Eyebrows said. "Where'd you leave those girls?"

Dutch had been dreading that question. He temporized. "They weren't in on our visit to Cosgrove's house," he answered hastily. "They just came along with us for a swim and a picnic."

"That wasn't the question, kid. Where'd you leave them?"

Dutch thought of Conawachie Beach, of Janet and Kathy safely surrounded by crowds of afternoon bathers and picnickers. It was a comforting picture. Surely nothing could happen to them there on a public beach in broad daylight. He said, "We left them on the beach by the inn."

"Is that all you wanted to know?" asked Cam incautiously, drawing another poke from Sal's gun.

"No," said Sal.

Just then the car halted near a small wooden maintenance shed that stood in a clearing near the side of the road. The planks of this shack, the boys saw, were old and weather-beaten but still sound. The shed was windowless; it had a flat roof covered with tattered tar paper; and it was set four inches off the ground by the two-by-fours on which the floor rested. An ill-fitting but sturdy door was held shut by a wooden pin pushed through the staple of an old-fashioned padlock hasp. Quite evidently the shack had served at one time as a tool and supply shed for the maintenance of this stretch of road, but it hadn't been used for years. The Plymouth's engine was switched off. The quiet of the woods descended on the clearing.

"Here we are," White Eyebrows said.

Sal went on as though he hadn't heard. "No. That's not all we want to know, kid. Unless the answer to both questions is the same."

Dutch frowned at Cam, but Cam was eying the rear-view mirror, watching Sal. Neither said anything. Sal said, "Is it? Is that where you left it? With the girls on the beach?"

"Left what?" asked Dutch.

"You know what," Sal said. "The suitcase. What else?"

There it was. Out in the open at last. Cam and Dutch had been pretty sure of it after their visit to Mrs. Cosgrove and impatient with themselves for not realizing it all along. That's what the whole thing had been about: the suitcase.

The suitcase, Dutch thought wearily. The old brown suitcase. The one his father had almost surely carried to Cairo four years ago, just as Mrs. Cosgrove had carried her car case to Cairo the same year. The old suitcase that because of its journey to Egypt had somehow, like Mrs. Cosgrove's car case, become an object of larcenous interest to these two men who now held Dutch and Cam at gunpoint.

Clearing his throat rather loudly, both to loosen its constriction and to serve as a warning signal to Cam, Dutch inquired with as great an air of innocence as he could muster, "What suitcase?"

"Suitcase?" Cam murmured in instant response to Dutch's lead, hopeless as it seemed.

Sal's thin lips curved in an unamused smile. The smile didn't reach his eyes, Cam could tell, watching him in the rear-view mirror. "You know what suitcase," Sal said, "and you'll tell us where it is. The easy way or the hard way. Take your choice."

"What suitcase do you mean?" Dutch asked, undeterred by the threat.

Sal replied patiently, "The one we couldn't find when we searched your jalopy just now while you were in the Cosgrove house. The one we know was in your car this morning at the gas station in Riverlawn."

"Why do you think I butted in at the gas station?" White Eyebrows seemed to be savoring his own cleverness. "To admire your stupid car? Huh-uh. To check on that suitcase."

"And that's why you tried to drive us off the road?" Cam broke in. "To steal some old suitcase you think we had?"

"That's it." Sal's tone was low and hard. "And listen, jerk, we know you had it." He nudged Dutch with the gunpoint. "We were parked near your house this morning. We saw your sister bring that suitcase down onto the porch for you. But you came by with your girl friends and picked it up before we could make a move."

Dutch felt a rush of guilt. Poor Hilda. She had been in real danger then, all because of him. His mother and his friends as well. He thought of Janet and Kathy. They were still in danger. It wasn't much comfort now to remember that he had extracted Joe Barry's promise of extra police protection for his family. For the crew of police car 17, assigned to keep an eye on them, hadn't prevented this black sedan from parking across the street from his house this morning and spying on Hilda.

In a desperate attempt to temporize further, he said, "That old brown bag you saw isn't worth anything at all. It's empty. We just brought it along to gather pine cones in."

As soon as he had said these words he could have bitten out his tongue. For he realized he had inadvertently told Sal and his companion what they wanted to know. If the bag was to be used for pine cones, it would be with Janet and Kathy—on Conawachie Beach. He hoped the implication of his statement would escape the two criminals.

His hopes, however, were dashed by the sly grin of triumph that overspread White Eyebrows' face, and by the sudden rasp in Sal's voice when he barked, "All right, kids. Out of the car." He emphasized this order with a wave of his gun. "And the bag better be on the beach with those girls."

Silently Dutch and Cam climbed out. While Sal covered them with his gun, White Eyebrows pulled out the wooden pin from the padlock staple on the shed door and pushed the door open. At the same time he drew from his pocket a large shiny steel padlock, brand-new.

Sal quickly searched the boys. He took only the scrap of paper bearing the Arabic addresses and the translation sheet from Dutch. He relieved Cam of a large penknife he habitually carried. Then he herded the boys into the windowless shed.

While the door was open, light from the outdoors illuminated the shack's interior enough for them to see that it was absolutely bare. Just a wooden box, fifteen feet long, perhaps, and seven feet high, empty, strong, seemingly escape-proof.

Cam's quick eyes examined every square foot of the walls, floor, and ceiling before the big door was pulled to by the men outside and the new padlock snapped into place.

With the closing of the door, the light was snuffed out as though by the sudden coming of midnight. The inside of the shack was as black as a coal pit, save where a tiny quantity of daylight filtered in around the ill-fitting door.

They were prisoners. It might take the police weeks to find them.

Dutch tried to still the quaver in his voice. He said to Cam in the darkness, "Now what?"

"Shhh," Cam answered in a whisper. "Listen."

He had his ear against the panels of the door. Outside they heard Sal's harsh voice say, "That ought to hold them. Until somebody lets them out."

"Yeah." White Eyebrows laughed. "And it won't be us. We got a date with a couple of other kids, now. I kind of liked that little blonde kid with the glasses, didn't you, Sal?"

Dutch whispered, "Janet!" in helpless fury.

"Not bad, the blondie," Sal said. "But the one with the black hair is more my dish."

Cam whispered, "They'll be safe on the beach, won't they, Dutch?"

"Sure. Hundreds of people around. Except"—and Dutch fought down his own panic—"the girls may be in the woods hunting pine cones all alone. I didn't think of that! And they might refuse to give the suitcase to these goons without an argument."

"They could get…get hurt, then, couldn't they?" Cam said.

Dutch nodded miserably, forgetting that Cam couldn't see him. "My fault. I gave the deal away to those two."

"Forget it," Cam said abruptly. "They already guessed it, even before you told. If we didn't leave the suitcase at Mrs. Cosgrove's, it had to be with the girls. Gee, I wish we had left it at Mrs. Cosgrove's!"

"So do I. Or had it with us, so we could just have handed it over to them. But we didn't know they wanted it."

"We know it now, buddy!" They could hear the two men talking together outside—in incomprehensible Arabic now.

Dutch said, "Those cracks about Janet and Kathy were for our benefit, Cam. To make us squirm. Maybe they won't bother the girls at all. Just grab the suitcase and hightail it out of Conawachie."

"Maybe. But we can't count on it."

"I know that. So I'm going to get out of here in a hurry!" Dutch began to prowl around in the darkness of the shed.

"What good will that do? Even if we escape, we could never get to the girls before those guys do. They've got a car, remember. We don't even have roller skates!"

Dutch put a hand on his friend's arm. "It isn't so far to the inn from here," he said in a whisper. "Not more than a couple of miles, if that."

"How do you know?"

"I snuck a look at their mileage when we left Cosgroves', and another outside just now. A mile and three quarters. And another half mile to the inn at the most."

"No kidding? That rough road seemed ten miles long to me!"

"About a mile. That's all. If we could get out, we could cut across country through the woods…"

Cam said in excitement, "That's right! We went north on Lake Drive to the rough road, then southeast to here. If we could cut across the hypotenuse of that acute angle to the inn…"

"What big words you use, Grandmother!" Dutch's spirits began to rise. "It took their car twelve minutes to make it from the beginning of the rough road to here. Add another five to get to the inn…"

"And we might beat them there if we could get out of here quick enough," Cam finished.

Outside they heard the starter of the Plymouth whirr and then the engine take hold. The motor idled for a moment. Sal called out. "Hey, kids!" His hoarse voice was sardonic. "One car a week goes over this road! Maybe you can make it hear you next Friday when it goes by—if you yell loud enough! Don't worry about your girls, though. We'll take care of them!"

And with this parting taunt they pulled away; soon the sound of the car's laborious passage over the potholes died out toward the lake.

"Quick!" Dutch said then, no longer bothering to whisper. "Let's take this place apart!" Rapidly he tested the strength of the shack's walls, threw himself against the door, stamped the planks underfoot to check the floor for weaknesses. "Everything seems pretty tight, Cam," he announced.

"Let me at the door," Cam said grimly. He backed off and charged as though he were diving through an off-tackle hole. He struck with a thud. The door didn't give an inch. They heard the padlock rattle, that was all. Cam rubbed his shoulder. Ruefully he said, "That dam padlock is stronger than both of us." He got down on his hands and knees, feeling for knotholes or cracks in the floorboards in which he might get a fingerhold to pull loose some of the planks.

Suddenly Dutch said, "The roof, Cam. That's our only chance."

"Right!" his friend agreed instantly. "The roof's just flat boards nailed down onto a two-by-four framework. I saw that when we came in. But I can't even reach the roof with my arms up, Dutch, and I'm taller than you are."

"If we could pry up a couple of those roof boards…" Dutch said. "Come over here to the wall, Cam." Cam felt his way to Dutch. Dutch bent down, placing his elbows on his knees for support. "Now see if you can crawl up on my back and reach the roof."

"A breeze," Cam said with enthusiasm. "You're a genius! Stand firm, now. Here comes a hundred and eighty pounds!" Lightly Cam clambered onto Dutch's bent back, balancing himself with hands on the shack wall until he had a firm foothold. Then he stretched cautiously upward. "Ah," he said. "Plenty of leverage this way!"

It took them two minutes, however, moving slowly along the shack's walls in their awkward human-ladder position, before Cam located a roof board that seemed to offer a possibility of escape. It was near the edge of the roof farthest from the door, and as Cam pushed mightily against it both boys could hear the protesting screech of nails being forced free of wood.

"Heave!" Cam yelled, exerting as much upward pressure as he could on the loose board-end. "Heave, Dutch!"

Dutch heaved. The end of the board came free of its joist with a harsh groan of rusty nails. Blessed sunlight streamed through the opening.

While Dutch slowly worked his way across the width of the shack with Cam standing on his back, Cam forced the loosened board upward all along its length until, in a shower of bits of tar paper, it finally snapped free of its nails at the other end, too.

Both boys whooped in triumph as the roof board was pushed aside to fall outside. "Quick!" Dutch panted. "The next board! That's only an eight-inch opening. We need a bigger hole!"

Cam pushed with all his strength against both ends of the neighboring roof planks. "No dice!" he gasped finally. "They won't budge. We'd need a crowbar." He jumped down from Dutch's back. "You've got to get through that hole, Dutch! Time's awasting!"

"What about you?"

"Forget me. Think of Janet and Kathy. I'll be all right. Anyway, who's the miler here, you or me? Get started!"

Cam stooped and grasped Dutch around the knees and lifted him. Dutch reached up, grabbed the edges of the eight-inch opening in the roof, and swung his legs forward and up to hook his toes on the edge of the long narrow opening. Then, with much grunting, scraping, and exhaling to ease the squeeze, he struggled through onto the cabin roof. In the tight passage he lost some skin off his forehead, tore a jagged hole in the back of his golf shirt between the shoulder blades, and ripped one of his hip pockets off his pants.

He looked down at Cam, who was standing below him, face uplifted, and said, "I'm out. I'll get to the girls. And we'll be back for you in a flash. Okay?"

"Okay," Cam said. "On your way, tiger. Remember you're the Flying Dutchman—and fly, man!" He lifted a hand. "See you."

Dutch slid to the edge of the roof, hung by his hands to avoid any chance of injuring his legs by jumping, and dropped softly to the ground.

Without even a backward glance at the maintenance shed he crossed the rutted road in a sprint, slipped smoothly into Iris reaching miler's stride, and plunged into the woods.

CHAPTER 12

Dutch Runs the Mile

Fortunately the floor of the centuries-old forest surrounding Lake Conawachie was relatively free from undergrowth. As Dutch dived into the green gloom under the pines he gave silent thanks that here, at least, only an occasional downed tree, scattered clumps of mountain laurel, and patches of baby saplings seemed likely to interfere seriously with rapid progress. The woods were open, the trees were rather widely spaced, and the forest floor was quite level.

Running easily, Dutch glanced at his wrist watch and tried to calculate the tune at his disposal if he were to beat Sal and White Eyebrows to Conawachie Inn. How long did he have? As the crow flies, the distance shouldn't be more than a mile or a mile and a quarter at most, he figured. That rough road from Lake Drive to the shed had angled south all the way and slightly east. So the shed ought to be about opposite the inn—only a mile or so farther east through the woods. It had taken twelve minutes to drive from the beginning of the rough road to the shed. And five minutes more would be a conservative estimate for the drive between Conawachie Inn and the north end of the lake, where the rough road joined Lake Drive. Say seventeen minutes, then, altogether. In a car. And the crooks had left on their return journey over the rough road approximately five minutes ago.

So that gives me twelve minutes or a little less to get through this woods and find Janet and Kathy, Dutch thought. He breathed an anxious prayer that his distance calculation was accurate. Twelve minutes! He settled down grimly to the business of running, his sneakered feet lifting and reaching in a graceful distance-eating stride. He lined out due west, surprised to feel sweep over him—even here in the depth of the woods—the wave of exhilaration that the start of a race always gave him. Subconsciously he paced himself as he would for a mile run on the cinder track behind Riverlawn High School.

Only here the track wasn't of cinders. It was softer, springier, more yielding to his feet, a mat of pine needles over rich loam. Dutch missed his running spikes. For the pine needle surface, although providing resilient footing, was dangerous in two respects: the needles were slippery, and fallen pine cones threatened a turned ankle at every step.

It was like running in a cathedral. The dome of foliage high above his head shut out most of the sunlight; the tree trunks flitted past him like the soaring columns lining a Gothic aisle. Watch it, Dutch told himself. Just run. Don't get fancy ideas about cathedrals.

He concentrated on running easily and without strain. He might have to last for more than a mile this time, he thought. His legs worked smoothly as though in oil. His effortless, machinelike stride carried him over the rough ground steadily; his feet seemed actually to grab the padded forest floor and pull it back to him, step by speedy step.

Save something, Dutch advised himself. Save something. Don't give it all in the first quarter mile. You've got plenty of time, stupid. Stick to your regular pattern. You beat that Lister in 4:32. That's a fast mile. Fast enough to get you to Conawachie Inn before that beat-up Plymouth. Maybe they'll break an axle in a pothole, anyway. Boy, what a break that would be! But don't count on it. Just run, Dutch. Rim like a rabbit.

He sneaked frequent looks at his wrist watch at first, then found this too distracting and concentrated on his running, his eyes picking out, and his feet mechanically avoiding, the obstacles that loomed ahead of him. So far he had experienced no breathing difficulty, no sign of growing fatigue or decreasing muscle response. He estimated he had run perhaps half a mile.

A pretty good half, too, he congratulated himself. Bet I did it in two-five. No, not with running around bushes and dodging pine cones. Maybe two-ten. Or two-twenty, even. What's the difference? If I'm halfway there now, I could crawl the last quarter on my hands and knees and still beat those two kidnapers to the girls! If! If I'm halfway there! I wish I knew how far it is!

Dutch set his mind on Janet as the best possible subject for thought to maintain his speed, fire his determination, and improve his morale. He pictured her—dainty, slender, satisfyingly feminine—lying on the beach at Conawachie Inn, listening to the radio while she tanned in the sun. Janet, Dutch assured himself solemnly, liked him. And he liked her. He liked her quiet humor, her down-to-earth common sense, the glasses that enhanced her Nefertiti look…

Abruptly he abandoned this line of thought because all at once he noticed that the woods had become thicker, the trees set more closely together, the ground more fully covered with second growth and underbrush. Huge deadfalls appeared.

His heart sank. He slowed down to a trot, desperately searching for openings in the brush and trees through which he could find a clear path in the right direction. For a hundred yards he struggled through the tangle, beset by mounting fears of getting confused, of losing his sense of direction in these featureless woods as he swerved time and again from his set route to avoid impassible thickets or closely set tree trunks that barred the way. The sense of swiftly passing minutes heightened his anxiety; his impulse was to run at top speed in any direction where he found a decent opening, hoping it would lead him into clearer country. But he sternly suppressed this desire, realizing that it was merely a symptom of approaching panic.

He looked at his watch. Disaster, in the form of its minute hand, stared him in the face. For it showed him that only five minutes of grace remained to him.

Dutch forced himself to be calm, although his every instinct drove him headlong toward desperation. He had to make the inn, he kept thinking over and over. He had to.

Just as he was about to give up in despair, he burst through a fringe of undergrowth and emerged onto a narrow footpath. The path wound crookedly through the trees, but it seemed to lead in the general direction Dutch wanted to travel. He paused only long enough to make sure of this before he resumed his long, loping miler's stride, his sneakers thudding on the firm, smooth surface of the footpath.

The path continued to lead him westward, widening and flattening a little. Dutch thought with a surge of hope that perhaps this footpath was one of the "woods walks" that the inn offered as an attraction to its guests—a forest hiking route that would inevitably lead directly back to the inn itself.

Dutch was running with his last bit of reserve drive now, fretfully conscious that he had already run more than a mile through the woods. Otherwise, why did his legs feel like hundred-pound weights that he manipulated awkwardly as if in a nightmare? Why was his breath sawing in his lungs, each inhalation a sharp cutting pain that caught him in the left side as well as the chest? And why had his famous last-quarter "kick," which had won him so many mile races, completely run out of juice at least a quarter of a mile back?

Dutch forced his weary legs to go on running. I can't let Janet and Kathy down, he thought. Or Cam, either. Wish I was a cross-country man! If I can only last till I reach the inn! If only I can get there ahead of Sal and White Eyebrows!

If, if, if. The forest seemed to lighten a bit before him. Without warning the trees thinned out. Suddenly he could see a log wall ahead at the end of the long funnel that was his path—a rustic log wall beyond a dark ribbon of asphalt that was surely Lake Drive! The rustic wall must belong to the inn!

Dutch's weariness and breathing pains left him as though by magic. It was like seeing the finish line ahead in a tight race. He felt strong again, fresh, full of go, confident that he could run another mile if necessary.

It wasn't necessary. He came out of the woods on Lake Drive, twenty yards to the left of the driveway that led to the inn's parking lot across the road. A quick glance up Lake Drive toward the north, a fast inventory of the parking lot opposite, showed him no black Plymouth sedan anywhere in view. Had it already reached the beach and gone again? Was he too late?

He snapped a look at his watch while dodging across the road and running down the beach toward the spot where Kathy and Janet should be. Two minutes of the twelve he had allowed himself still remained. His heart lifted.

He came in sight of the girls' beach blanket. The radio was there. He could hear it playing softly, some kind of South American tune with lots of strings. The girls' short, terry-cloth beach robes were there, too, cast carelessly on the blanket with their beach towels. But the girls were nowhere in sight.

Neither was the old brown suitcase.

Dutch reached the deserted blanket, but he didn't pause there. He veered left toward the fringe of woods that backed the beach, separating it from the road. If the girls were gathering pine cones, they'd be in those woods. Somewhere nearby, Dutch prayed. And if Sal and White Eyebrows had already been here, had found the girls in the woods alone... Dutch didn't like to dwell on that possibility. Bathers on the beach were looking at Dutch's running figure with curiosity. He ignored them. There was no time even to solicit their help.

Slowed to a stumble, he followed two sets of footprints that dimpled the dry beach sand from the girls' blanket to the edge of the woods. Only two sets of footprints! Dutch was weak with relief.

Inside the forest fringe he stopped, leaned panting against a tree, and called as loudly as his ragged breathing allowed. "Janet! Kathy! Are you here?" He thought he caught a blur of movement among the trees to his right, twenty yards in from the beach. "Janet! It's Dutch!"

Janet's cheerful voice caroled through the pines. "Here we are, Dutch. Are you back already?" Her carefree voice was one of the most welcome sounds Dutch had ever heard in his life.

He started toward it. The girls came to meet him. Janet had the brown suitcase in one hand.

In their bathing suits and beach slippers the girls looked young and beautiful and gay. And most especially, Dutch added to himself thankfully, they were safe and unmolested. So far.

He said with a snap in his voice, "Janet! Dump the pine cones out of that bag and take it out to your blanket on the beach. Quick!"

"But we've only just filled it..." Janet began.

Dutch cut her off. "Please do what I say, Jan! Then run back here as fast as you can. Leave the suitcase on the blanket. Please!"

"Where's Cam?" Kathy asked. Dutch ignored her.

For only an instant Janet hesitated, taking in Dutch's skinned forehead, his torn shirt, his labored breathing, his air of desperate urgency. Then, without another word, she snapped open the suitcase, dumped its contents unceremoniously on the ground, and ran out of the woods onto the beach. She put the empty suitcase down on the blanket beside the radio. Then she hurried back into the woods to rejoin Dutch and Kathy.

"Now, then," she said eagerly, "what's this all about, anyway?"

"Where's Cam?" Kathy repeated insistently. "Isn't he with you?"

"Let me get my breath," Dutch said. "Cam's okay—but come here a minute." He drew the girls back into the woods a little further, then led them fifty yards north toward the inn. Here, hidden from view of anyone on the beach, they paused while Dutch found a vantage point among the trees from which they could see the spot on the beach where the suitcase stood on the girls' blanket.

"If Cam's all right, where is he?" Kathy was anxious. "Tell me, Dutch!"

"I'll tell you in a minute," Dutch answered soothingly, peering out at the beach.

"What are we waiting for?" This was Janet.

"The two men who tried to ditch our car today. They should show up any second out there. That's why you had to take the suitcase out on the beach just now. I couldn't take a chance they'd see me, because I'm supposed to be locked up in a shed two miles away. They want that old suitcase. And they play pretty rough, Cam and I found out. So we're going to let them have the suitcase and welcome to it!" Impulsively Dutch put an arm around Janet's shoulders and finished, "Gee, I'm glad you're both okay!"

Behind her spectacles, Janet's blue eyes regarded him warmly but with bewilderment. "Of course we're okay," she said. Then suddenly, "Did those two men do this to you?" She touched his scraped forehead.

"In a way. But they threatened you and Kathy, too, which is much more important." His voice tightened. "Quiet! Here they come!"

As nonchalant as any aimless vacationers taking an innocent stroll on the beach, Sal and his henchman suddenly appeared, making their way through the clutter of bathers unhurriedly, and casting searching glances around them as they came. They were headed directly toward the girls' beach blanket.

When they spotted the scuffed leather suitcase, Dutch saw a change come over them. They quickened their pace a little; they stopped turning their heads from side to side to scrutinize the beach and the bathers; they set a straight course for the old brown suitcase, like bees returning to a honey tree.

"They've seen it!" Kathy whispered. Then she did a double take. "But that little man hasn't got white eyebrows, Dutch!"

Dutch murmured, "I'll tell you about that later, too."

Sal reached the suitcase. They could see him bend over it, examine it closely, seize the handle in one hand and heft the bag lightly. Then he nodded to White Eyebrows in evident satisfaction, said a few words to him, and with unbelievable arrogance calmly seated himself on the girls' beach blanket and rested one hand affectionately on the suitcase while his partner walked back down the beach toward the inn.

"How do you like that for nerve!" Dutch said. "He's waiting for the little guy to get their car so he can just duck through the woods out to the road with the bag and not have to carry it down the public beach to the parking lot!" Dutch seethed with anger. Sal took out a cigarette and lighted it, blowing placid plumes of smoke into the summer sunshine.

"Do you suppose they'll try to find Kathy and me now?" Janet said.

Dutch shook his head. "Not as long as they've got the bag. That's all they want. But oh, boy, am I glad I got here before they did!"

"What do they want with that old suitcase?" asked Kathy.

No wonder they were puzzled, Dutch thought. But they weren't any more puzzled than he was. What did Sal and White Eyebrows want with his father's old suitcase? He shrugged. "Save it, Kathy, huh?" he begged. "Let's wait till those thugs go before we start to kick that question around. Okay?"

"Well," Kathy murmured rebelliously, "okay. But I still want to know where Cam is and whether he's all right."

Presently they heard the sound of a car passing down Lake Drive behind them. The squeak of brakes told them that it had pulled up. And at the gentle beep of its horn Sal tossed aside his cigarette, picked up the suitcase by the handle, and faded inconspicuously into the woods, heading toward the road and his waiting confederate. If Dutch and the girls had stayed where they were when they first met in the woods, Sal would have run right into them.

Dutch wiped a hand across his damp forehead. "Whew!" he breathed in immense relief as Sal disappeared, "I hope that's that! If I never see those babies again it'll be too soon!"

They heard the Plymouth out there on the road behind them start up. And soon the sound of the car's southward passage was swallowed up by distance and the woods between.

CHAPTER 13

Danger in Duplicate

It was three o'clock when Dutch climbed out of Cam's jalopy at the old shed in the woods and beat a thunderous tattoo on the plank door.

"Hey, Cam!" he called through the door. "The Marines are here! Are you still in there?"

A calm, untroubled voice answered from beyond the panels. "I'm still here, pal. Where'd you think I'd be? Did you get to the girls in time?"

Kathy, at Dutch's shoulder, said through the door, "Oh, Cam, are you all right? Dutch told us about everything…"

"Kathy! You okay? Swell! I am too. Not a hair out of place. But I'm awfully glad you and Janet didn't run into those Arabs! You didn't, did you?"

"We saw them," Janet chimed in, but we didn't meet them. They took the suitcase, Cam. Dutch barely had time to warn us before they showed up on the beach!"

"Good boy!" Cam said. "That kid can travel, can't he? Even though he's so little he can squeeze through an eight-inch hole? How about getting me out of here?"

Dutch laughed. "Wait'll I get your jack handle."

Without even pausing to change from their bathing suits, Janet and Kathy had insisted on accompanying Dutch back to the forest shack to release Cam. Kathy's dark eyes had been pools of worry, despite Dutch's assurances that Cam was perfectly all right. They had hurried to the parking lot at the inn and hired the hotel taxi to carry them at once to Mrs. Cosgrove's house on Lake Drive, where Cam's jalopy was still parked.

There Kathy had taken over: fishing under the right front fender of the jalopy where she knew Cam kept a spare ignition key taped to the metal; jumping with alacrity into the driver's seat and starting the motor; then, with Dutch and Janet crowded in beside her, driving the jalopy northward with as much flair and verve as Cam himself could have displayed.

Dutch didn't offer a word of objection; he knew how anxious Kathy was about Cam and realized that taking direct physical charge like this would keep her occupied until her fears were relieved. So Kathy had driven them at a suicidal pace over the ruts and potholes of the abandoned road, and as they drove, Dutch had filled the girls in on the events of the past hour. It seemed almost incredible to Dutch that such a short time span could encompass all the things that had happened since their arrival in Conawachie.

He thrust the narrow end of Cam's jack handle through the hasp of the new padlock White Eyebrows had put on the shed door. Taking a good grip on the steel rod, he threw all his weight on it. There was a snap like a pistol shot. The padlock broke open.

"You can come out now, Mr. Osborn," Dutch said to his friend.

Blinking in the sunlight after the darkness of the shed, Cam grinned at Dutch and said proudly, "You really made it, you Dutchman, didn't you?"

Kathy was standing anxiously before him in her bathing suit. Without speaking, she reached out and took one of his hands in both of hers. Cam squeezed her hands reassuringly, patted her bare shoulder, and said to Dutch with unmistakable sincerity, "Thanks, pal."

"Any time," Dutch said lightly, a little embarrassed. "I needed the exercise."

"Tell me about it," Cam demanded.

They piled into the jalopy. "Back to the beach," Dutch directed.

"The Arabs didn't take our picnic basket, too, did they?" Cam asked. "I could eat a horse!"

"What a relief!" Janet said. "Now everybody can relax. The Arabs have surely gone for good. They have the silly old suitcase. And that's apparently what caused all your troubles, Dutch."

Contentedly reclining on one elbow on the beach blanket, Cam was still gnawing on a chicken leg, the last of their picnic lunch. Arguing that all danger from Sal and White Eyebrows was now over, Dutch had insisted that they go through with the afternoon's program exactly as planned—first, the swim, and then the picnic on the beach afterward. It was now four o'clock, and ever since Cam's release from the cabin in the woods they had discussed sporadically and to little purpose the mystery of the old brown suitcase and Mrs. Cosgrove's stolen car case.

"The only thing I can figure out," Dutch had said, "is that there was something very valuable in my father's old suitcase when he brought it home from Cairo. And those Arabs knew about it and were determined to get it."

"Then there must have been something very valuable in Mrs. Cosgrove's car case too," Janet suggested. "Something she had brought home from Cairo."

"Sure," Cam said. "It figures."

Kathy shook her head stubbornly. "Not to me, it doesn't. That suitcase of Dutch's was empty, Cam. Janet dumped all her pine cones out of it. It was empty. And the men knew it was empty, because the tall one shook it to find out."

"That's right, Kathy." Dutch thought for a moment, then said, "So anything concealed in the suitcase—or in Mrs. Cosgrove's car case—would have to be hidden in the lining, or the corner rein-forcements, or the handle, or the hardware, or someplace where it would never be discovered unless you knew where to look."

"You couldn't hide anything very bulky," Cam protested.

"It doesn't have to be bulky. Suppose it's jewels, or flat sheets of platinum, or…or dope," Janet said. "Yeah. That would be possible, I guess."

"Or," Dutch said after a long pause, "five golden fingernail covers from the tomb of King Tut-ankh-amen of Egypt."

Cam stared at his friend. "The false fingertips? They were swiped from the museum, Dutch. If that's what the Arabs were after, they got them at the museum. They wouldn't be looking for them in your Dad's old suitcase."

"They got fake fingertips at the museum. Dr. Kilty is certain of that."

"So? You mean they thought they were real when they stole them?"

"Maybe. Without examining them closely, you couldn't tell they were just gilded lead. They looked like the real thing in our display case."

"And when the Arabs found out they'd stolen a set of phony fingertips, then they decided the real ones were in your Dad's old suitcase?"

"I don't know." Dutch was solemn. "But it could have been something like that."

"It's crazy," Janet said, "because the tall one tried to break into your house and steal the suitcase before the museum robbery, Dutch."

"I can't explain it." Dutch grinned. "Anyway, I'm sure of one thing. They wanted that suitcase. The fake TV man tried to steal it from my house; they nearly killed us today in the car, trying to get it; and they took the chance of stealing it off our beach blanket right here in broad daylight, in public." He paused, hearing in memory Hilda's pert voice saying, "He had black eyebrows that stuck out like bushes." Dutch snapped his fingers and added, "They even tried to buy the suitcase from Hilda, by golly! She mentioned a short, bushy-browed secondhand dealer who came around to the house offering cash for old gold, old luggage, and stuff. I bet that secondhand man was White Eyebrows—with black ones!"

"They wanted the suitcase so badly that whatever's in it must be priceless," Kathy said. "Would your Pharaoh's fingertips—if they were genuine, that is—be priceless, Dutch?"

"Darn near, Kathy. Genuine original Egyptian antiquities of pure gold and more than three millenniums old, would be worth"— he paused—"almost anything you could imagine."

"Who'd buy them?" Janet asked. "Stolen antiquities that were known to be stolen?"

Dutch laughed. "Any number of private museums. Any number of wealthy but unscrupulous collectors. Those five fingertips from King Tut's tomb would be the gem of any private collection. There might even be a collector somewhere who would commit murder for them!" Dutch stopped abruptly.

"Murder is right," Cam said. "And kidnapping, too. And assault and battery."

"The Arabs themselves aren't collectors, I'm positive of that," Dutch said slowly. "They wouldn't know a funerary temple from a hole in the ground."

"Me either," said Cam.

"Anyway," Janet said, "they aren't working for the Egyptian government or anybody respectable, that's sure."

"Maybe they're working for themselves," Cam said. "Whatever they find in suitcases and car cases they sell to somebody who is a collector." He grinned at Dutch. "Unscrupulous, that is."

Dutch nodded. "That's the most likely idea."

Kathy said, "I don't want to appear forward, people, but it seems to me that the sixty-four dollar question hasn't been asked yet."

"That's right, it hasn't." Dutch laughed and made a grandiloquent gesture with his hand. "So you ask it, Kathy."

"Well," Kathy said, "if there is something valuable from Egypt in your father's old suitcase, Dutch, and in Mrs. Cosgrove's car case, how did it get there?"

"Bingo!" said Cam. "The jackpot!"

"I wish I could answer that one." Dutch frowned at his hands. "I know my father didn't have anything to do with it. And I bet your Mrs. Cosgrove didn't either."

"Absolutely not," Cam said. "She was as much in the dark as we were about it."

"So we'll probably never know," said Dutch with regret, "whether it was our Arabs that put the treasures into the luggage in Cairo or somebody else. Or how they did it. Or how they expected to trace down the valuables in America. Certainly the two pieces of luggage we know about aren't the only ones involved."

"Which reminds me," drawled Cam with a pretense of boredom. "While I was sitting in that shed with nothing else to do, I did a little thinking."

"You were thinking?" Kathy put a hand on his forehead. "Do you feel well, Cam?"

"Still a bit hungry," Cam returned, "but otherwise top-hole. As I was about to remark when I was so rudely interrupted…"

Kathy threw sand on the chicken leg he still held in his hands.

"I got a faint glimmering of a possible explanation of those funny letters and figures on the scrap of paper, Dutch."

Dutch said eagerly, "No kidding? The code stuff written after each address?"

"Yeah. Take that first one, after your name. What was it again?"

"1A2F3W." Sal had taken the scrap of paper from him at the shed, but Dutch knew he would never forget that particular sequence of numbers and letters.

"1A2F3W," Cam nodded. "That's it. Now follow me closely, kids. Professor Osborn only lectures once!"

"So start lecturing," Dutch urged.

"Okay. That scrap of paper we found was torn off the top of a list of names and addresses, right?"

"Right."

"And your name and address, or your fathers, rather, was first on the list. Right?"

Dutch nodded, absorbed.

"Therefore, the number 1A opposite your name might conceivably mean that on list number one your name was item A. Do I make myself clear?"

Dutch grinned. "As mud, bud. You mean these guys may have had three lists, numbered one, two, and three?"

Cam beamed. "Exactly. You get it right away."

Janet said, "I don't, Cam. I'm sorry. Is that all?"

"That's as far as I could get," Cam said. "I don't think well unless I'm eating, and my stomach was empty at the time." He looked at Dutch. "Do you think it's possible?"

Dutch said slowly, "It could be. Say the Arabs have three lists. What could they be lists of? No trouble about list number one. It's a list of names and addresses, written in Arabic. But what could list number two be?"

"What?" asked Cam obligingly.

Dutch said, "Almost anything. But maybe it's a list of the jewelry, or the dope packages, or the platinum sheets, or the antiquities or whatever they're after. How about that?"

"It sounds reasonable," Janet said, encouraging him.

"All right. Now on that list, whatever's in my father's suitcase might be the sixth item, mightn't it? Or letter F, in other words. That would account for the first four digits of the code 1A2F after my dad's name."

"By George, I think maybe you've got it, Dutch!" Cam sat up. "And the third list; what would that be, do you suppose?"

Dutch said, "The third list could be descriptions of pieces of luggage, maybe, where valuables were hidden, or exactly where in the luggage the stuff was, or something of that sort."

"That makes a lot of sense," Cam commented. He muttered the code number under his breath, "1A2F3W. That could mean: Oscar Schildecker in Riverlawn owns an old brown leather suitcase twenty by sixteen by eight inches, with five gold fingertips from King Tut's tomb concealed in the corner reinforcement patch!"

Dutch grunted and shook his head. "We're probably dreaming," he said.

"And why three lists, anyway?" Kathy asked brightly.

Janet spoke up. "That's easy. If they were written in Arabic, all three of them, and each kept in a different place, anybody who happened to see one wouldn't realize what it was—or care. And all by itself it couldn't incriminate anybody, either. It would be Greek to anybody but another Arab with the code." She looked at Dutch. "Even the police."

Dutch said guiltily, "We should have showed our paper to Joe Barry, though." He began to help Janet pick up the picnic debris and pack it into the hamper. "Who's for another swim before we change to go home?"

Cam rose and stretched. "I am. I think I can outswim you this time, Kathy. But it'll make me hungry again, I'm afraid." He laughed and added casually, "After all this excitement over your old brown suitcase, Dutch, I'll never feel comfortable again carrying our track gear in the other one."

Dutch froze. He paled and stared at Cam, stricken. And Cam, already starting for the water's edge, halted in mid-stride and slowly let out his breath in a soft whistle. "Oh, my gosh!" he said then.

Janet looked from Dutch to Cam. "What's the matter?" she asked. "What other suitcase are you talking about?"

Dutch pounded his forehead with the palm of his hand in disgust. In a barely audible voice, he said, "Talk about morons! I'm the world's worst! I completely forgot about that one, Cam!"

"What one?" Kathy demanded.

"The other suitcase of the set. My father had two, just alike. One of them we brought along today. The Arabs took it. But the other one, its twin, is at Cam's house. We've been using it for years to carry our stuff in when we go on athletic trips!"

Janet realized the significance of that shattering statement before Kathy did. She turned a troubled face on Dutch and said, "Oh, Dutch! How awful! That means we may not be rid of the Arabs after all!"

"That's exactly what it means, I'm afraid," Dutch agreed.

"Why?" asked Kathy.

Cam, who had been struck temporarily dumb by his own casual remark, now said in sheepish apology, "Some brain I've got! That other suitcase never even entered my head!"

"What's so bad about it?" Kathy said.

"Figure it out this way," Cam explained. "If Dutch's dad took two suitcases, just alike, to Cairo with him, there's a chance that whatever the Arabs are after could be in the one at my house—and not in the one they just stole from us."

Kathy's mouth rounded in dismay.

"And," said Dutch, picking up the reasoning, "that's not all. There could be valuables in both suitcases, for all we know. So the Arabs could want them both." Janet said quietly, "I don't think so, Dutch. I don't think there could be valuables in both of them."

"Why not?"

"Because of the way the Arabs talked to you about the suitcase, as though there was only one. They made no reference to there being two, did they?" Janet smiled. "Remember there was only one code notation beside your address on the list."

Slowly Dutch nodded at her in admiration. "That's solid thinking, Jan. They didn't mention another suitcase to us, did they, Cam?"

"Not that I remember."

"All the same, it's bad enough that they've taken the wrong one, maybe, by mistake. Because that would mean…" Dutch hesitated.

Cam finished for him, "…that they'd still be after us, to get the other suitcase—when they find out they've goofed."

They were silent for a moment, thinking hard. The girls watched Dutch anxiously. At last he said with an air of uneasiness, "Look. Say they got the wrong suitcase today. Say they've found it out by now. What's their next move?"

"Go after the other bag," Cam said promptly. "Hotter than ever. Because now we're onto them. We can identify them. We can tell the police what they're up to. So they'd have to move fast."

Dutch said, "If they don't find what they're after in the bag they just stole, they'll figure pretty quick that there must be another suitcase just like it, at my house. Either that or they'll think their list is wrong."

"But the other bag's at my place," Cam said. "So why worry? The Arabs can't possibly know that. Not if they didn't know till now that there are two suitcases."

Dutch said, "The Arabs won't know the other bag's at your house, you're right. So they'll head for my house again. Fast. And here I am, a hundred miles away! And Mother's working. And Hilda's likely to be home alone, unless she's over at Rita's or at the movies or somewhere."

"I see what you mean," said Cam bleakly. "Let's find a telephone."

While the girls were changing out of their swim suits Dutch telephoned home from the inn.

He waited impatiently until the distant bell had rung a dozen times. There was no answer. "At least Hilda isn't there alone," Cam said. "Call your mother at the store."

Dutch pondered. "No," he said finally, "we're just guessing about this, and if there's nothing to it, I'd be scaring Mom for nothing."

"Let me try my house, then," Cam said. "My mother and dad have flown to New York to meet Aunt Gunvor's ship from Norway, but Ruthie, our cook, ought to be there."

"What will you tell her? To beware of strangers looking for our track bag?"

"Sure. And to try and locate Hilda and warn her, too."

"Swell," said Dutch. He surrendered the phone to Cam. Cam called his home in Riverlawn.

There was no answer.

"I can't figure that one out," Cam exploded. "Ruthie ought to be there!"

They looked helplessly at each other. "Let's call Joe Barry," Dutch said then.

Cam cheered up immediately. "Sure! We should have tried him first!"

"We should have told him about that darn scrap of paper, too! He'll be burned up."

"Who cares? Call him!"

So Dutch put in the call. Police headquarters in Riverlawn reported, impersonally, that Sergeant Barry was off duty and couldn't be reached for at least an hour or so.

Cam, who was pressing his ear close to the receiver, following Dutch's conversation, hissed, "Tell them to alert that police car in your neighborhood!"

Dutch said to the police operator in Riverlawn, "This is Dutch Schildecker, calling. Sergeant Barry promised to have police cruiser seventeen keep a sharp watch on my house on Seventeenth Street, officer. Could you send out a call to that cruiser to be especially alert for the next few hours?"

"Sure," the police operator said. "But what's it all about?"

"Sergeant Barry knows," Dutch said. "And it's too complicated to explain over the phone. Just tell Sergeant Barry I called from Conawachie, will you? And tell him, when he comes in, that I'll be home in a couple of hours. And that we've got news for him about the museum robbery. You won't forget to call car seventeen, will you? It may be nothing, but it could be important."

"Okay."

Dutch said thanks and hung up. He turned to Cam. "Let's get out of these swimming trunks and head for Riverlawn, Cam." He looked at his watch. "The Arabs only have about an hour-and-a-half's start on us."

"Only! That's plenty on a little hundred-mile drive." Cam grinned. "But let's see how fast that old crate of mine will really go, shall we?"

"What are we waiting for?" Dutch said.

CHAPTER 14

Cam Breaks the Law

As it turned out, Cam's jalopy could go pretty fast.

They hit Route 71 doing a smooth mile a minute; and on the straight stretches of that twisting highway Cam cajoled the speedometer needle up to seventy. It was still too early for heavy traffic, a fact for which the boys were thankful.

"Don't run us into a culvert or anything, pal," Dutch warned his friend. "Remember we have a couple of ladies along."

"How could I forget?" Cam laughed, turning his head toward Kathy, whose dark hair was blowing wildly in the wind. "And I, for one, think a lot more of them than I do of any old suitcase."

"Thanks a lot!" Janet murmured. "How flattering."

"Keep your eyes on the road, please, Cam," Kathy said seriously.

"How do you like that, Dutch? A back-seat driver, yet!"

"After all," Kathy said, "we can't afford to take chances at this point with *Hilda's* safety, either."

Dutch sobered. "Gee, I hope she's over at Rita's or at the movies. And stays there till we get home."

"How about your mother?" Janet asked. "Doesn't she come home for dinner?"

"Not on Saturdays. She stays at the store straight through till ten. Eats dinner at the store cafeteria."

"I'm sure Hilda will be all right," Janet reassured him. "There's at least a fifty-fifty chance that the Arabs got the right suitcase this afternoon. And if so, there's nothing more to fear."

But at that moment they passed the spot on Route 71 where Sal and White Eyebrows had attempted to force their car off the road; and remembering the Arabs' cynical disregard for their possible injury or death, Dutch found it difficult to discard his qualms about Hilda's safety. He was certain the thieves would go straight to his house in their search for the other suitcase—if they searched for it at all.

Presently they turned off Route 71 onto the three broad concrete lanes of Highway 37, which was crowded with Saturday afternoon traffic.

"Now," muttered Cam, "we'll be able to open this thing up a little."

The jalopy seemed to take wing. It swept over into the passing lane of the highway, brushed with effortless ease past a dozen cars going in the same direction, and took off for Riverlawn like a homesick swallow heading for its nest.

"Hey!" yelled Cam in wild exuberance, "open the gate, Agnes, here comes the Riverlawn Rocket!"

The speedometer needle was quivering uncertainly on seventy-nine when the siren sounded behind them.

* * * *

"I'm sorry," Cam apologized sheepishly as they followed the police car at sedate speed into the hamlet of Petrole, fifteen minutes from Riverlawn. "Now we'll be later getting back to Riverlawn than if we'd just stuck to the speed limit all the way."

Dutch was worried, but he said nothing to upset Cam further. He merely shrugged. "This won't take long, I hope. And maybe we can telephone home from here and raise somebody this time."

They drew to the curb behind the police car, which had stopped in front of a red brick house. The words *Justice of the Peace* were lettered on a sign in the living room window. Four other cars were parked nearby, but otherwise the tiny village seemed completely deserted.

The uniformed officer who had caught them speeding climbed out of his car, came back to their jalopy and said to Cam, "All right, son. Come in here with me. It's your car?"

Glumly, Cam nodded.

"I won't need the rest of you, then." The traffic officer was heavy-featured, stolid, obviously bored.

"Is there a phone in there I can use?" Dutch asked him.

"No need to yell for a lawyer before you're hurt," the officer said, smiling.

"It's not for a lawyer. It's an important personal call."

"I'm afraid there's no phone inside you can use." The man looked up and down the street. There wasn't a public telephone booth in sight, not even a store or a gas station that might have a telephone. "And I'm sorry, but regulations are that you can't move this crate until Junior, here, pays his fine," the policeman said. He jerked a thumb at Cam. "We shouldn't be long, though."

Leaving Dutch and the girls in the car, Cam climbed out and disappeared with the officer into the house. Janet touched Dutch's arm in silent sympathy.

When Cam returned, fifteen minutes later, he looked both chastened and relieved. "Fifteen dollars fine," he told them as he climbed behind the wheel. "That must be how Petrole gets its major revenue—from traffic fines like that. There was a crowd in there. When it came my turn, I pleaded guilty to speeding. Then I was given a ten-second lecture on how lucky I am not to have my license lifted. And then told to pay fifteen bucks on the barrelhead or get thrown in the clink. It was as cut and dried as an assembly line."

"Did you try to call Riverlawn?" Janet asked.

"Nope." Cam started his engine. "I figured it would probably be a waste of time by now. If the Arabs were going to Dutch's house, they'd have gotten there already. And it'd be too late to warn Hilda. I say we ought to get home as quick as we can. How about it, Dutch? You want to find a phone here or go on to River-lawn?"

"Let's get home," Dutch said. "I hope Hilda wasn't there if the Arabs arrived, that's all."

The remainder of their journey to Riverlawn was accomplished in less than half an hour despite heavy traffic and their care not to risk any more entanglements with the law. It was 6:45 as they drove into the outskirts of town.

"I'll take you home after we've checked at Dutch's house, okay?" Cam said to the girls.

"Of course!"

They turned into Seventeenth Street. "I don't see that darn police cruiser," Dutch said. His voice reflected his uneasiness.

With a jerk Cam set his parking brake, and they all piled out of the jalopy and ran for the front door of Dutch's house. Dutch's eyes were busy as he ran. Nothing seemed disturbed. No signs of forcible entry or violence. The house seemed peaceful and untenanted. When he found the front door closed and locked as usual, Dutch breathed a sigh of relief and got out his door key.

"I guess Hilda's not here. And the house looks as though the Arabs haven't been here either."

"Good!" Janet said happily. "They did get the right suitcase, then. I'm so glad!"

Dutch turned his key, pushed open the front door. He immediately raised his voice in a shout. "Hilda! Hilda!"

They waited but heard no answer. Dutch called again without result. He cast hurried eyes around the downstairs rooms, saw nothing amiss.

Cam looked into the kitchen. "Everything okay here," he reported.

Janet and Kathy were standing in the hall. "Look upstairs, too, Dutch," Janet said, "just to be on the safe side."

Cam and Dutch went up the stairs, three at a time. They separated at the top of the steps, Cam bursting through the open door into Hilda's bedroom, Dutch looking into his own room and his mother's.

"Okay here!" Dutch called. "Anything there, Cam?"

Cam didn't answer immediately.

With a feeling of foreboding Dutch scrambled down the hall and looked into Hilda's room. What met his startled gaze seemed at first to confirm his worst fears.

Hilda was lying on her wildly-disordered bed, fully clothed. Her ankles were tied together with twisted strips of cloth torn from the bed sheets. Her wrists were fastened securely to the headposts of her bed. A damp yellow washcloth had been stuffed into her mouth to serve as a gag.

Cam was leaning over the bed, talking in a low reassuring voice to Hilda and struggling to unknot the binding strip about her head that held the gag in place. It wasn't until Dutch saw Hilda's wide-open excited eyes following Cam's every movement with adoring admiration that he knew she was all right.

"Hilda!" He hurried to the side of her bed. "What happened?"

Hilda, still gagged, could only roll her eyes at him.

Dutch ran to the head of the stairs and called down to Janet in a voice he tried to keep steady. "Janet! Will you telephone the police for me right away? The phone's in the dining room. Try to get Joe Barry."

"Is…is Hilda up there, Dutch?"

"Yes! Tied up on her bed! The Arabs have been here after all!"

"Is she hurt?" Kathy was almost afraid to ask.

"I don't think so. Call Joe, Janet. Ask to have somebody sent over here right away."

Dutch turned back to his sister's room.

Hilda, released now from her bonds and gag, was sitting on the edge of her disheveled bed. The gaze of transparent hero-worship she was directing toward Cam was slightly sickening, Dutch thought.

Kathy arrived in the doorway in time to hear Hilda's first words. Hilda clasped her hands at her breast. "Cam saved me!" she said, fluttering her eyelashes. "Isn't he gorgeous?"

Kathy raised her eyebrows at Cam. Cam blushed.

* * * *

Sergeant Joe Barry and another officer, both in plainclothes, reached the house within a few minutes. Hilda was just saying, "I came home from the movies at five o'clock to get my supper ready…" when Barry and his man unceremoniously pushed into the living room.

"What's this all about?" Barry barked, his bafflement making him brusque. "Who was tied up? And by whom? And what was that call from Conawachie…"

Hilda interrupted him. "It was me," she said primly. "I was just telling Dutch—"

"Tell *me*," Barry said. "And make it fast."

With her eyes occasionally going to Cam to see how he reacted to her story, Hilda told what had happened to her. "At about five-thirty the doorbell rang and I went to answer it, and it was a little man with white eyebrows who said he was from the electric company and pushed right in. I tried to stop him, but he came in and shut the door and grabbed me. He put a hand over my mouth so I couldn't scream and then pushed me upstairs and tore my sheet to absolute ribbons and tied me up on the bed. Honestly I was so scared I thought I'd simply die! He put that washcloth in my mouth—ugh!—and then went to the attic, and I could hear him moving around up there for several minutes. Then he came downstairs again to my room and he was furious. I could tell that. And he jerked the washcloth out of my mouth, and he asked me where that old brown suitcase was—the one that belonged to Father, Dutch. I told him you took it up at Conawachie Lake to gather pine cones in. He said 'No, not that one, the other one just like it.' I couldn't think at first where the other one was, and he threatened to burn my wrist with his cigarette!"

Hilda shivered delicately, watching Cam from the corner of her eye. When he clenched his jaw at this information, she smiled secretly to herself and went on, "But then I remembered where the other old suitcase was and told him. When school closed, Dutch, you said Cam took your bag home with him. So I told the man that. Then he stuffed the cloth in my mouth again and left. He didn't really hurt me at all."

Joe Barry burst out, "Where were those rabbit-brained men in car seventeen while all this was going on! They had their orders to watch this house."

Cam said, "I'm going to call my house. We can find out about car seventeen later. If Hilda told the Arabs the bag was at my house…"

"Arabs?" Joe asked.

"Yeah, Arabs." Cam turned to Hilda. "Did you tell him my address?"

She nodded, crestfallen. "I'm sorry, Cam, but I really had to. He was going to burn my wrist…"

Cam went to the telephone. Ruthie, the Osborn's maid, answered on the third ring. "Ruthie," Cam said urgently, "has anybody been there within the last hour or so about a suitcase?"

Cam listened intently to her reply and then said, "Tell me about it, quick!" More talk from Ruthie. Then Cam: "So they got it, eh? By the way, where were you at four o'clock, Ruthie? Nobody answered the phone when I called. Oh, I see. No, nothing's wrong. Be home pretty soon."

"They've got the other bag," he said to Dutch as he hung up. "About half an hour ago. A tall guy posing as the janitor from the museum came and told Ruthie you had sent him to pick up that old bag of yours with your track clothes in it. Said she had no reason to doubt him, and gave the man your bag. Just like that. She was out in the backyard watering the roses when we telephoned her earlier. Didn't hear the phone."

"Listen, Joe," Dutch said to Sergeant Barry, "that means these two Arab crooks are only half an hour ahead of us!"

"Arabs?" asked Joe again.

"The guys that robbed the museum," Dutch said. "The guys that conked me. They're also the guys who tied up Hilda, and stole two suitcases from me, and kidnapped Cam and me at Conawachie today, and threatened us with a gun…"

Barry stared at Dutch, gaping slightly. Finally he stuttered, "They wh…what?" Then he snapped, "But that can wait! Do you happen to have any idea what these…ah…Arabs will be likely to do next, now they've got this suitcase from Cam's house?"

"They'll scram out of Riverlawn," Cam stated.

"The Plymouth!" Dutch turned to Joe. "A black Plymouth sedan, current model four-door, rental car, license number VM-113! That's what they were driving, Joe! Maybe they'll…"

Joe Barry said to his companion, "Get on the phone, Jerry. Put that car on the wire. All-points alarm. Did you get the number?"

Jerry nodded, running for the phone in the dining room. "And tell them to alert all city police on it," Joe ordered. "I want that car." He asked Dutch, "Give me a description of the short guy. You already told me about the tall one, I guess. He was your TV man, right?"

"Right. But a description's no good, Joe. These fellows wear disguises. They could look like almost anybody now."

"Then for heaven's sake," Joe urged, "bring me up to date on what's been happening! I thought I was supposed to be handling this case. But everybody else seems to know more about it than I do!"

So Dutch and Cam, taking turns, told Sergeant Barry everything that had happened to them in Conawachie, everything they had discovered in their amateur sleuthing, everything they suspected. Barry listened without interruption, save for shaking his head at intervals and muttering "you should have told me" several times. When they came to their enforced trip at gunpoint to the maintenance shed at Conawachie, he said, "Hold it!" and told Jerry to get on the phone to the local FBI office and ask if Mr. Curtin could come around to Dutch's house immediately.

"There's no use running off in all directions until we know where we are," Joe said. "We'll wait for Curtin. The theft of Egyptian government antiquities, if that's what it is, and their kidnapping of American juveniles ought to give the federal government an interest in these Arabs of yours, too. And the FBI wouldn't thank us for messing up the trail before they get on the job. I hope Curtin's available. He's a good man."

Barry's man returned from the telephone to report that Agent Curtin would be at Dutch's house in ten minutes.

CHAPTER 15

Enter the FBI

Agent Curtin proved to be a slender, pleasant, steel-spring sort of man with a low voice and an authoritative manner. He had worked with Sergeant Barry before, and liked him. It needed only Barry's mention of international theft and kidnapping to kindle his immediate interest. And within ten minutes of his arrival at Dutch's house he had absorbed their whole story in astonishing detail.

He was inclined to agree with Dutch's analysis of the Arabs' actions. "Obviously," he said, "something valuable was concealed in Schildecker's suitcase and Mrs. Cosgrove's car case. Probably stolen Egyptian antiquities, possibly almost anything smallish in size. And obviously, too, these Arabs knew specifically where to look for each particular piece of luggage, which tends to support your theory of descriptive lists." He paused. "But I'm more inter- ested right now in catching these men than in figuring out their motives and methods. If you could only give me a little more to go on! One of them's tall with hunched shoulders, and the other one's short with merry eyes! What a description!"

Dutch said, "I wish we could do better. But their other features kept changing, sir."

Curtin said, "Your fake TV man, the taller Arab. He spoke with a trace of accent?"

"Yes, sir. They both did."

"He was half bald and had brown hair?"

"Yes, sir."

"That was probably his own hair. But today he wasn't bald? He had black hair?"

"That's right. Crewcut. A full head of it."

"So he wears a toupee, then. Okay. Now. Hunched, thin shoulders, every time you've seen him?"

"Yes. Even in the museum the night he hit me."

"That's what gave Dutch the identification originally," Barry broke in. "Hunched shoulders."

Curtin nodded. "Any other differences in the tall one's appearance the other two times you saw him, Dutch?"

"Well, he wore dark glasses as the TV man, but today, no. His clothes were almost the same, both times. Except he didn't wear a cap today."

"His face?"

Dutch closed his eyes and tried to remember. "Maybe his face seemed a little bit broader and fatter the first time. Yes, I'm sure it was. His cheeks were practically hollow today, weren't they, Cam?" Cam nodded.

"All right. He could have used pads or lumps of wax inside his mouth to make his cheeks look fatter and his lips thicker. It's an old trick. Now, the short man?" Hilda said timidly, "When he pretended to be a secondhand man that time, he had bushy black eyebrows and a straight, beautiful nose and a darling little black mustache…"

"And today," Cam said, "he had white eyebrows first, with a straw hat hiding his hair and no mustache. Next he had black, close-cut hair and smooth black eyebrows and still no mustache."

"I didn't recognize him when he came today," Hilda offered. "But now I think of it, his nose was still straight and beautiful, so…"

"Dark, swarthy skin," Dutch said. "And kind of plump cheeks. Today, anyway."

"All right," Curtin said. "Now. Keeping toupees and false eyebrows and mustaches in mind, think back, Dutch. The Arabs must have kept pretty close tabs on your house and on you for quite a while. Did you ever notice anybody who *could* have been one of these men hanging around your house or following you?"

Dutch said slowly, "Not consciously. I wasn't really looking for anybody, of course. At least not until the museum robbery when I thought I recognized those hunched shoulders on the tall thin man."

Cam, sitting between Kathy and Hilda on the sofa, jerked up-right abruptly and had opened his mouth to say something when he saw from Dutch's expression that he, too, had suddenly been struck by the same arresting memory.

"Cam!" Dutch exclaimed. "How about that night at Cox's after the track meet?"

Cam nodded. "I was just going to say. The guy you saw looking in the window…"

"I thought he carried his shoulders kind of hunched."

"But you said he had fatter cheeks than your TV man. I thought it was Fatty Duveen at first, remember?"

"What's all this?" Curtin asked. "*Did* you see somebody who could have been the tall Arab?"

Dutch said, "The same day the TV man tried to get into this house. I thought I saw a guy who looked like him watching me through Cox's window. Cam and I followed him home. But he turned out to be an innocent citizen."

"What made you so sure of that?"

"Because we found out he wasn't bald. And he had a fatter face and thicker lips than the TV man. But we didn't know then about these disguises…"

"He was even whistling a hootchy-kootchy tune!" Cam said. "Like—Arab music!"

Curtin stood up. "You followed him home. Where?"

Dutch said, "Doheny's Hotel. Jefferson Square."

"Come on!" Curtin said. "It's worth a try."

Dutch said uncertainly, "What about the girls?"

"Kathy and I will stay here with Hilda till you get back," Janet said. "We'll be all right now. Don't worry. Hilda feels fine."

"Thanks," said Dutch. Then impulsively, with a smile at her, "Gee, you're wonderful, Jan."

"So's Cam Osborn," murmured Hilda very softly. "Yum!"

Dutch grinned, then turned and ran out of the house to the curb where the others were already getting into cars.

* * * *

In the golden light of early evening Doheny's Hotel on Jefferson Square looked even more shabby and rundown to Dutch and Cam than it had on their previous visit.

Curtin led the way briskly into the hotel's dreary lobby.

The desk clerk, a middle-aged man with a hacking cough and a myopic squint, stood idly behind the untidy desk. At his back was a wooden rack of numbered mail slots.

Curtin said, "Federal agent," and flashed his badge briefly. "I think you have two guests we want."

The clerk's eyes rounded. "Federal agent? Does that mean the FBI? My! My! You don't tell me!" He peered nearsightedly at Cam, who stood at Curtin's shoulder. "And aren't you the star halfback of Riverlawn High's football team, young man? I've seen every one of your games, do you know that? For the past two seasons…"

"Thanks," said Cam, interrupting, "but…"

"And I have a season ticket for next fall, too!" the desk clerk concluded triumphantly. "I enjoy football *so* much!"

"These guests," Curtin said. "A tall hunched man, thin face, brown hair, partly bald. And a shorter, plumper character with happy eyes, black hair, black eyebrows. Both with a slight foreign accent. Probably sharing the same room. Ring any bells?"

The desk clerk was seized with a paroxysm of coughing. When it subsided, he wiped his eyes with a soiled handkerchief and nodded brightly. "Of course. That's Mr. Jacob Allen and Mr. Salem Fay. With us for about three weeks. We don't have a full house, just now, and I happen to know those two quite well. Very nice gentlemen, both of them. No trouble at all." Inevitably he asked the question: "Why? Have they done something illegal? Surely…"

Curtin said, "We think so. We want to find them in any case. Are they here now?"

The clerk shook his head. "I'm sorry. They checked out half an hour ago."

Dutch groaned in disappointment. So close!

Curtin held out a hand. "Give me your telephone," he asked the clerk.

The clerk passed it across the desk. Curtin said to Sergeant Barry, "Here, Joe. You already passed the word on the black Plymouth, I know. Now see if you can set up something with your people to cover trains, airplanes, and buses, too, eh? In case the Arabs ditch the rental car and try something else?"

"Sure," said Joe. "Easy. Only with such vague descriptions of them—and them being disguise artists, apparently…"

"Do the best you can, okay? Meanwhile, I'll take a look at the room where these birds lived." Curtin turned to the clerk. "What room?"

"Nine. The room's open. Second floor. You'll have to walk up, though. We have no elevator." The clerk was apologetic.

"I guess we can make it," Curtin said. He motioned for Dutch and Cam to follow him.

They ascended the stairs together. Room 9 was the first room on the right of the landing at the rear of the hotel. Curtin strode to it, twisted the unpolished brass doorknob. The door opened. They crowded into an empty, depressing hotel room like a million others. A single glance sufficed to tell them that it probably contained nothing to assist them in their manhunt. Dresser drawers, closets, ashtrays, wastebasket—all were empty.

They began to search the room nonetheless. The only sign of recent occupancy they found, besides the mussed bed, was lying on the floor, half concealed under a throw rug at the foot of the washbasin. It was a scrap of black silky hair fixed to a thin cloth backing and coated with spirit gum.

Dutch, picking it up, said "Here's the little guy's false mustache."

Curtin nodded and slipped the mustache into his jacket pocket.

"You think they'll get away, Mr. Curtin?" Cam asked.

"They won't get far. They feel too safe to need to try anything fancy. After all, they think you two are still locked up in a shed a hundred miles away."

"And Sergeant Barry's men will block them from leaving town?"

"Sure. They'll cover everything. Buses, trains, planes, autos."

"But suppose the Arabs have got away somehow, between the time they left this hotel and now? Before the airport and stations and roads are covered?"

Curtin shrugged easily. "That'll just be a little bit harder. We'll still get them."

Dutch reached up a hand and felt the back of his head reminiscently. "I want to be in on it when you do," he said. "I owe those Arabs something. They knocked me out. They mistreated my sister. They threatened me with a gun…"

"Oh, brother!" Cam said, his eyes flashing. "Wouldn't I like to get a crack at them!" He clenched his big fist and hammered it against the wall, making the dirty windowpane rattle in its frame.

Curtin looked amused. "Take it easy, son," he said. "Leave it to us." He turned serious then, and his voice took on a faint tone of reproof. "That's what you should have done all along, you know, boys. Left it to us."

Dutch flushed. "Yes, sir," he admitted. "I guess that's right."

"Forget it," Curtin said, something new in his voice. "Come here a minute, Dutch."

Dutch went over to stand beside him. Curtin was staring out of the room's one window. It was of the old-fashioned double-hung type. The bottom sash was raised a foot from the sill. "Look," Curtin said, "down there in that court." He pointed.

Cam said, "What is it?" and started across the room toward them.

Dutch took a quick look down into the grimy courtyard at the back of the hotel. "My suitcases!" he cried then. "Both of them!"

Curtin lifted the window sash all the way up and leaned out the window. "Brown leather. Just alike. You sure they're yours, Dutch?"

"Sure," Dutch said, leaning out. "Positive."

Cam looked, too. "The handle's gone from one," he observed.

"So that's where they hid it!"

"Hid what?" Curtin asked, smiling.

"Whatever they were after. In the handle of my father's old suitcase!"

Curtin nodded.

"Yeah," said Cam, "because the handle of the other one has been cut off at one end, like they were looking for something in it first."

Curtin said, "You do talk like detectives, at that. I apologize for thinking you were merely amateurs." He grinned at them; they could detect no hint of irony in his tone. "Looks as though the Arabs got what they wanted in the second suitcase handle, all right. Cut it off the bag and threw the two suitcases out the window."

"Why?" Cam said.

"To get them out of sight and out of their hair, I suppose. The handle was all they wanted. And they're no doubt traveling light."

"Wonder why they came back here to the hotel after they got the second suitcase at Cam's house?" Dutch said.

"I'd say to pick up whatever it was they stole from Mrs. Cosgrove's bag. They probably had it stashed here." Curtin started for the door. "Let's go down and have a closer look at those bags."

Joe Barry met them at the top of the staircase as they left room 9. He said quietly, "They'll cover the terminals. And while I was talking to headquarters they told me a call had just come in for me on my first alert."

"Hey!" Cam cried exuberantly. "You've caught them?"

"Not the Arabs. The car. The black Plymouth."

"Where is it?" This was Curtin.

"One of our boys spotted it in the parking lot out at Riverlawn Airport."

"Good work," said Curtin. "Let's get out there. You two boys come, too. We may need you to identify these Arabs for us."

The two cars left Doheny's Hotel together. Joe Barry's police car led the way, bearing Joe and his fellow policeman, Jerry. Then came Curtin's inconspicuous unmarked Ford in which Dutch and Cam rode with the FBI man.

They barreled down Jefferson Square's bumping like two beetles on a dirty leaf and turned north toward Main Street.

Before leaving Doheny's for the airport, Curtin had asked Sergeant Barry, "Your men are at the airport now?"

And Sergeant Barry had rejoined, "Sure. We have a team there all the time. One of our regular airport detail spotted the Plymouth. All headquarters had to do after my call was give the airport boys descriptions of the Arabs. They're being looked for, don't worry."

"I'm not worrying," Curtin had said. "Just checking." Curtin drove with the same smooth polish that characterized his voice and manner. He glanced sidelong and with amusement at the stiff, tense position in which Dutch was holding his wiry body. "What's the trouble, Dutch?" he asked. "We're heading for the last round-up now. The pay-off to any piece of good detective work—catching the crooks. Aren't you ready to enjoy it? The way I see it, you and Cam have done most of the detective work on this case."

"I'm ready, all right. And I'll enjoy it." Dutch relaxed. "But a guy can't help it if he's a little nervous, can he?"

"Nervous?" said Cam from the back seat. "I'm shaking like a leaf! I just hope these monkeys don't get away from us! Boy, I'll make that little happy-eyed Arab wish he'd never left the Nile!"

"How about the tall one?" Curtin said, deadpan.

"I'll leave him to Dutch," Cam replied, grinning.

"My buddy," Dutch said.

"Although," Cam went on, "I might be able to take him, too—if somebody'd hold his gun while we wrassle!"

Suddenly in dead earnest, Curtin said, "I'll repeat what I said back there in the hotel. Leave this to us. I mean it. If we latch on to these Arabs, it's possible somebody could get hurt. I don't want it to be you. Understood?"

"Okay," said Dutch, "if you say so."

"I say so. How about you, Cam?"

"Okay." Cam was silent a moment, then laughed. "Unless I'm attacked. Then I may have to defend myself."

Ahead of them the police car was traveling fast. Joe hadn't turned his siren on, though. He wanted to come into the airport quietly, to institute his search for the fugitives without alarming other travelers or forewarning the Arabs.

Curtin's car kept up with effortless ease. Cam said with the natural curiosity of a boy with a souped-up car of his own, "Is this baby fixed for you, Mr. Curtin?"

Curtin said, "It'll go pretty good if I need it." He caught Cam's eye in his rear-vision mirror. "But I never hurry it unless it's a real emergency, Cam. You shouldn't either, you know it? How many days' work on the road gang did that fine cost you in Petrole?"

"Two," Cam said sadly. "Fifteen bucks. Gone the way of all flesh." He sighed. "But my Daddy done told me, as the song says. I was out of line."

"I'll pay half the fine," Dutch said. "You were speeding on my account."

Cam shook his head. "Huh-uh." He laughed. "I was speeding on Hilda's account…" He looked ahead. Joe Barry's car was turning into the airport entrance.

CHAPTER 16

Action at the Airport

Sweeping up to the curved portico of the clean marble building, Curtin braked to a halt immediately behind Barry's cruiser and stepped out of his car, followed by Dutch and Cam. The three approached Joe Barry, who had been met at the airport terminal's door by a uniformed policeman who was now talking earnestly to him.

As they came up Joe turned to Curtin and said with satisfaction, "We've got 'em. O'Brien, here, says the Plymouth is over in Parking Lot Four, but that he thinks he's spotted one of our men in the lunchroom having a sandwich and beer."

"One of them?" asked Curtin.

O'Brien nodded. "The little one," he said. "Haven't located the other one yet. But after all, it's only been ten minutes since headquarters gave us the word on them."

"I'd say you've done great to locate even one of them in just ten minutes," Curtin hastened to compliment him.

Mollified, the airport policeman said to Barry, "Don't worry, Sergeant. We'll get the other one, too. He's here, all right. Bound to be."

"How can you be sure?"

"Because the first thing we did when we got orders not to let these two Arabs on a plane was to go around to all the airlines' ticket counters here and check their passenger lists and recent requests for space. This is Saturday night, see. And everything's booked solid. We figured that unless your men had reservations in advance, which wasn't likely, they'd try to get space on the first plane they could—right here."

"Good figuring," Joe Barry said. He gave O'Brien an approving nod.

"So what do you think we found?" The man was enjoying his dramatic moment. Dutch and Cam fidgeted impatiently. "All four airlines that have planes going out of here tonight for New York have listed two guys on their waiting lists within the last half hour. The same two guys in every case. A Mr. Fay and a Mr. Allen."

"Funny they'd use the same names they used at Doheny's Hotel," Barry said.

"Why?" asked Curtin. "They don't know we're after them. They don't know we've been to Doheny's. They think Dutch and Cam are still out of touch in Conawachie, locked up in a shed."

"That's true," Barry said. "Anyway, if the Arabs are listed as stand-bys to get the first canceled or no-show space on a New York-bound plane, they're both here, all right."

"Sure. And the beauty of it is," said the airport cop, not to be deprived of his triumph, "that if these boys are going to leave Riverlawn by air tonight, they'll be paged over the public address system! How do you like that for a quiet getaway? They'll be asked to report to whatever airline counter has got space for them. So we just listen for their names to be announced, then stroll over to the proper airline counter and pick them up as they check in, no matter what disguise they're wearing!"

Joe Barry clapped his airport colleague on the shoulder. "Like shooting fish in a barrel!" he said. "Good work, O'Brien! You say the short one's in the lunchroom?"

"I think," said O'Brien. "Not sure. Corresponds in some ways to your description. I spotted him myself, five minutes ago. But he's all alone. Haven't seen anybody come near him. And if they're together, you'd think…"

"Basic precaution, maybe," Curtin said. "To avoid each other's company in public places."

"Let's take a look at him anyway," Barry said. Dutch and Cam breathed a sigh of relief. They'd been afraid the police would stand in the airport door arguing non-essentials forever. "Or," said Barry, deferring to Curtin and dashing their spirits again, "do you want to wait out of sight until they're paged and take them both then?"

"We'll look now." Curtin was brisk. "One at a time is easier than both together, I always say. And they might not be paged for hours. Come on, kids," he said to Dutch and Cam, "but hang back. All we want you to do is identify this lad."

Dutch and Cam followed the officers into the terminal lobby. The lunchroom, gay with gold and red drapes and a gold-starred ceiling, was on their right. Dutch punched Cam's arm and said, "Here we go, Sherlock!"

"I need my pipe and deer-stalker hat." Cam grinned. His muscles were tight with excitement. "Otherwise I'm ready to wind up your case for you, Watson!"

They were approaching the lunchroom door. "If," said Dutch, "this is really White Eyebrows they've spotted in here."

The blonde cashier, seated behind her high boxlike desk, didn't even look up as the six stood quietly for a moment under the arched doorway of the lunchroom, inspecting the room's occupants.

"Over there at the counter," O'Brien said in Barry's ear. "The guy with the red mustache and eyebrows and the too-big hat. With the plaid suitcase beside him. The mustache and eyebrows could be false, like you tipped us. The rest of him corresponds pretty good, don't you think?"

Barry said, "Yeah. Thanks, O'Brien. Keep an eye out, you and the other boys, for the tall skinny one now, okay? We'll handle this one." He turned to Curtin. "You want to? Or shall I?"

"I'll do it," said Curtin politely. "But I want to be sure of my bird, first." He motioned Dutch and Cam to step up beside him. "Is that him?" he asked, jerking his head toward the oblivious beer drinker at the counter, whose profile was toward them.

"I think so," said Dutch immediately, "but it's hard to be sure from the side. I'll go around and take a seat near him, shall I? Where I can see his face better? Then, if he's the right man, I'll give you the sign, Mr. Curtin. Will that be all right?"

"I'll go with you," Cam said instantly.

Curtin said, "One's enough. Go ahead, Dutch. We'll stay here out of sight until you give us a nod or a head shake."

Dutch sidled into the lunchroom and went quickly toward the other end of the wide counter that stretched along one wall. He kept his face turned in apparent search for an empty table, so that the short man at the bar wouldn't glimpse it. There seemed slight chance of that, however, as the red-browed man, unaware of any danger, was giving his undivided attention to his sandwich and beer. Probably the first food he's had since breakfast, Dutch thought.

He took a seat at the counter two stools removed from White Eyebrows. A fat middle-aged lady with a flowered hat occupied the intervening stool, affording him partial screening. He picked up a menu and pretended interest in it for a moment, slumping down behind the fat lady's ample silhouette.

All at once Dutch was uncomfortably aware that he had no disguise, that he would be recognized immediately if White Eyebrows should happen to lift his eyes from his sandwich and glance his way. And if that should happen, what then? Dutch asked himself. The fat would be in the fire for sure. For seeing Dutch—not a hundred miles away, as he thought him to be, but here in the Riverlawn airport lunch room—White Eyebrows would realize his peril instantly. He'd know the police were upon him. Ready to pounce. In his anger what violence might he not attempt? Dutch felt decidedly nervous, despite the presence of Agent Curtin and Sergeant Joe Barry.

Then he told himself not to be stupid. Was that man two stools away really the Arab with the beaming, merry eyes? That's what he was here to decide. So Dutch leaned back on his stool, looked past the fat lady, and made a bold examination of her neighbor with the red eyebrows. He couldn't see whether the man's eyes were characteristically beaming and merry, or as sad as King Lear's on the moor, because the man was wearing a pair of cheap dark glasses with white frames.

But Dutch didn't need to see his eyes to identify the short Arab with certainty. For the false red eyebrows were ragged and bushy, just as the black ones and the white ones had been. On close inspection the red mustache seemed too sharply defined along its edges to be genuine. Dutch noted the dark skin, the coconut straw hat. He recognized the dark suit by its shiny elbows and knees, even in the artificial light of the lunchroom. And most convincing of all, he could see on the man's left hand—wrapped now around his beer glass—the same bitten, deformed thumbnail he and Cam had noticed on the hand with which White Eyebrows had steered the black Plymouth in Conawachie.

Dutch turned full toward the lunchroom archway and nodded his head up and down with great vigor.

Immediately Curtin strolled through the arch and approached the red-browed man at the counter. He stood behind him, leaned negligently forward, and said something softly in the man's left ear. At the same time he placed a hand on the man's right shoulder and held his FBI badge forward in his other hand for the man to see. Then he motioned easily with his head, slid a hand under the man's arm, as though he were a friend who had come to tell him he was wanted on the telephone, and drew him unprotesting and unresisting toward the lunchroom door. As they passed Dutch's stool Curtin said softly, "Bring his suitcase."

Not a soul in the restaurant save Dutch realized that an arrest had been made.

The expression on the Arab's face, as nearly as Dutch could judge, was that of a man stunned by unexpected disaster. For the moment shock robbed White Eyebrows of all initiative, all power to think. He went with Curtin like a docile drunk.

Dutch felt exultation rise in his throat as they disappeared together. He slipped from his stool, picked up the Arab's suitcase from the floor next to the fat lady, and scurried out of the lunchroom, waving a hand to the puzzled waitress who had just come up to take his order.

In the concourse outside the lunchroom door, Curtin was saying to Joe Barry, "Put the cuffs on him, Joe. And have your man hold him in your car outside until we see about his partner, eh?"

Barry nodded. "But first, Mr. Allen," Curtin went on in his unemphatic voice, "where's Mr. Fay? Your partner. The tall man called Sal. Where is he?" As he spoke he gently stripped away a bushy red eyebrow from his prisoner's face. It came away easily. With one red eyebrow and one black, the Arab had the look of a clown.

Securely held by Barry and his henchman, White Eyebrows merely stared blankly through the smoked windows of his sunglasses at the FBI man, trying to recover his wits, working desperately to discover some way, any way, out of this sudden catastrophe. Finally he said, "Find out for yourself, G-man." He made a sour grimace with his lips as he saw Dutch emerge from the lunchroom door with his suitcase.

"Thanks, Mr. Allen," said Curtin unruffled. "I'll do that." To Jerry, Barry's man, he said, "Take his suitcase to the car, too, will you?"

Leaving O'Brien to watch the lunchroom in case Sal should seek out his partner there, the rest entered the main lounge and waiting room of the air terminal. They looked over the people in the vast rotunda carefully. Curtin told Dutch and Cam, "You'll be able to recognize the tall Arab better than we will. Remember, he could be almost anyone, now. Maybe even a woman."

"Look for Miss America," Cam said, laughing. "She'll be an ugly skinny dame with big feet and hunched shoulders and a face that would stop a clock!"

They walked slowly through the main lounge and the waiting rooms, then inspected the shops and amusement arcades. They looked in every restaurant, club room and office, but nowhere did they see anybody who could have been the Arab, Sal, even skillfully disguised.

At length Curtin said to Sergeant Barry, "Even if he saw us taking his partner and was warned by that, he couldn't get out. He's here somewhere."

"But where?" Cam said. "We've covered the whole place and not a sign of him."

Barry said, "The airport detail's looking for him, too. He must be so well disguised his own mother wouldn't know him."

"Let's try again," Curtin said.

They covered the terminal once more, without success. Headshakes from Barry's men as they met and passed them confirmed that no one had found a trace of Sal.

"Okay," Curtin decided at length. "Into the field cocktail terrace. We'll be able to check every departing plane passenger from there while we're waiting for the loudspeaker to call Mr. Salem Fay."

Dutch spoke up. "Mr. Curtin," he said, "Sal must have seen us by now. He wouldn't know you or Joe by sight, maybe, but he sure knows Cam and me. And when he saw us, he'd know we were after him."

"Sure. And so?"

"So we won't find him in one of the public rooms. Disguised or not, he'd be pretty sure Cam and I could pick him out."

"You think he's hiding in a private room someplace, then, is that it?"

"Yeah," said Dutch.

Barry said, "We've looked in the washrooms. They're private."

"How about the ladies' washrooms?" Cam said, grinning. "You said yourself, Mr. Curtin, that Sal may be made up as a woman."

"True," Curtin said, amused. "The kids are right, Joe. The Arab can't possibly get away from us. But we may save ourselves a good deal of time by digging him out now. If he knows we're here, he may not even answer the loudspeaker call, of course. So tell your men to check the ladies' washrooms, will you?"

Barry nodded. "How about you?"

"I'm going to see the airport manager to get a line on other possible hiding places in the building." Curtin turned to Dutch and Cam. "Meanwhile, you two sit down right here and wait for us, okay? And keep your eyes peeled for Sal. He might show up."

"Shall we grab him if he does?"

"Yell for us, I told you. He's got a gun." With that, Curtin went off toward the main lounge again, accompanied by Barry.

Dutch and Cam sat down on a bench to wait as instructed.

They were in a corridor of the terminal building that led from the rotunda to an exit on the parking lot outside. This corridor was lined on both sides with display booths, glass-fronted, containing exhibits that advertised local industries. Neon signs were glowing now in these display windows, red, blue, and green, setting up flickering patterns of light in the corridor.

Diagonally across the corridor from the bench where Dutch and Cam sat, a narrow opaque glass door bore the legend Airport Displays, Inc. in gold letters and led into a small office, now dark. The advertising staff of Airport Displays, Inc. had quite obviously called it a day and gone home.

Dutch felt Cam's elbow in his ribs. In an electric whisper Cam said, "That door over there. It's not closed."

"Airport Displays, Inc., you mean?"

"Yes. Look at it. The office is dark. But the door's not even latched."

Dutch felt his neck hairs prickle. Green neon replaced red in the flashing sign behind him, but even in the rainbow lighting

Dutch could see clearly that the door to Airport Displays, Inc. was indeed not pushed to. It was resting against its latch.

"That's funny," he whispered back.

"Do you suppose…?" Cam began, then stopped as abruptly as though his tongue had been suddenly paralyzed. For across the corridor the door to Airport Displays, Inc. was slowly being pushed open. They watched, spellbound. Very gradually the door crack widened to two inches. And yes, there could be no doubt of it: the neon sign, now red again, was being reflected in the moist mirror of a human eye, set close up against the inside of that crack and peering through it.

Somebody was lurking in the deserted office of Airport Displays, Inc. and reconnoitering the corridor through the crack in the door—somebody who didn't want to be seen. Somebody who had reason to resort to stealth. Somebody who could only be a tall, hunch-shouldered Arab named Salem Fay!

Both boys tensed on their bench. The Arab hadn't seen them yet; they were seated outside his narrow line of vision as he scanned the corridor. Both Dutch and Cam sensed at the same instant that Sal, if he found the corridor was clear, meant to make a break toward the parking lot exit and take his chances among the crowding cars outside.

Putting a hand on Dutch's arm, Cam rose silently from the bench. He drew Dutch up with him. They softly crossed the corridor in two strides and took up positions against the wall on one side of the gradually opening door. They looked up and down the corridor, hoping for sight of Curtin, Joe Barry, or any policeman. But the corridor was deserted.

The door beside them was halfway open now. The top of a dark crewcut head appeared around the edge of it. The head twisted to look down the corridor toward the rotunda. Sal still didn't see the boys poised motionless behind the door.

Thinking the corridor clear, he suddenly erupted from the Airport Displays office in a clatter of pounding feet.

Automatically, without conscious purpose or volition, but driven by an overpowering urge simply to prevent Sal's escape, Dutch called out breathlessly, "Wait! You'll never make it!"

It was Sal, all right, who spun around with a snarl as Dutch's cry rang out in the echoing hall. His eyes were murderous when he saw Dutch and Cam.

He cast one agonized hopeless glance toward the door of his dark sanctuary and slapped a big hand into his jacket pocket. It was an incredibly fast, deadly reaction. There was no moment of stunned surprise for Sal as there had been for White Eyebrows.

But Cam's reaction was even faster. Explosively he launched himself at Sal's ankles in a flying tackle. His arms were outstretched, ready to enfold Sal's legs on contact. He knifed through the air like an animated projectile. And as the gun came free of Sal's pocket, Cam's charging shoulder took Sal in the shins and slammed him to the marble floor of the corridor with a jarring, sliding crash.

"That tackle was something to see!" Dutch told everybody later. "A real Osborn special! It caught me flat-footed—I almost forgot Sal had a gun!"

"Almost," Cam added. "Dutch almost forgot the gun. But not quite. The minute I knocked the Arab off his pins, Dutch was jumping on the wrist of his gun hand with one foot, and kicking the gun out of his hand with the other! You should have seen that little gun travel! Only the door at the end of the corridor kept it from ending up out in the parking lot!"

As it turned out, the two boys had selected, purely by instinct, the safest and most efficient method of disarming their desperate quarry. Sal, after losing his revolver to Dutch's mighty kick, seemed to collapse like a punctured tire. Perhaps he was merely stunned; perhaps where surprise had been unable to confound him even for a moment, Cam's bruising tackle on a marble floor had done the trick. When Agent Curtin and Sergeant Barry came running down the corridor a few seconds later, drawn by the commotion, Sal was making only token attempts to dislodge Cam's arms, which were clamped like iron rings around his legs, and fight his way to his feet. And he was paying no attention whatever to Dutch, who was dancing around the prostrate pair, waiting for a chance to land a solid blow to help Cam subdue the enemy.

"All right, all right!" Curtin snapped, smiling at Dutch's antics in spite of himself. "Don't kill him, boys! Take it easy now. Joe and I will handle him." He reached down and pulled Cam off Sal's body.

Cam said, breathing hard, "It was self-defense, Mr. Curtin! Honest."

"I believe you."

Joe Barry got out handcuffs, snapping one cuff of the pair on Sal's wrist, the other on his own. "Now that we got him located," he said with a grin, "I'm going to know where he is, from here on."

All Sal would say in the police car on the way back into Riverlawn was a gruff apology to his partner, White Eyebrows, "The stupid gun caught in my pocket lining!"

What had made the gun catch, however, was not Sal's pocket lining. It was the curved leather handle of Dutch's old brown suitcase. They found it in Sal's gun pocket when they searched him at the airport.

"Here," Curtin said to Dutch, handing the handle to him, "this was the reason for the whole thing. You might as well look at it, Dutch. It's your suitcase handle, after all."

So standing in the flickering reflection of the neon advertising signs with Cam, Joe, Curtin, and Sal looking on, Dutch up-ended the hollow piece of stiffened leather and shook into his cupped hand five small objects.

They were pointed circlets of rich pure gold, soft enough to be dented by a thumbnail. The satiny patina of age made them glow warmly in Dutch's palm. They were set irregularly with lovely studs of carnelian and lapis lazuli and turquoise.

Dutch bent his head over them and said with awe in his voice, "King Tut's fingertips!"

Joe Barry, gaping, said, "Not the ones stolen from Fulmer Museum!"

Dutch shook his head. "Oh, no," he said, "not those. They're fakes. These are the genuine, three-thousand-year-old articles!"

CHAPTER 17

A Visit from Mr. Stone

That was Saturday night. The week that followed was a ka-leidoscope of shifting excitements for Dutch and Cam. Although both their names had frequently appeared in the headlines on local sports pages, neither Dutch nor Cam was really prepared for the bold, front-page publicity that now overtook them.

They were interviewed exhaustively by the press. They had their pictures in the papers, flanked by such headlines as *Local Athletes Foil International Thieves; High School Boys Capture Criminals; Riverlawn Lads Recover Antiquities*. It seemed to Dutch and Cam that Joe Barry and Agent Curtin, in giving the story of the Pharaoh's fingertips to the press, had rather gone out of their way to award major credit for the recovery of the antiquities to Dutch and Cam—and especially to Dutch. This was puzzling but pleasant.

Even Hilda, Kathy, and Janet came in for their share of atten-tion in the news, since they, too, had been deeply involved in the thrilling events. And Dr. Kilty, bursting with pride that a young member of his own staff should have been personally responsible for the recovery of two world-famous Egyptian antiquities, accept-ed with gratitude the fine publicity the Fulmer Museum received as a result. Yes, *two* antiquities—for among a tangle of soiled apparel in the suitcase Dutch had appropriated at the airport, Curtin and Barry had found a flat, bejeweled royal necklace of heavy gold that was obviously another genuine relic. This one, they assumed, had been the unsuspected treasure in Mrs. Cosgrove's car case.

Dutch and Cam made two visits to Joe Barry's office at police headquarters, where they dictated, as best they could, a detailed account of their recent adventures. The police stenographer then typed up the statements and asked Dutch and Cam to sign them.

When he went to work on Monday, Cam was accorded a new brand of respect by the members of his construction gang—they were almost as friendly to him as though he'd been a pick and shovel man for years and not just a high-school football player. And Dutch won instant popularity with the museum employees by willingly describing, on request, his impressions of the priceless gold fingertips he had actually held in his hand and giving a blow by blow account of his part in the museum's own small robbery.

Cam's parents, with his aunt from Norway, arrived in Riverlawn on Sunday afternoon to find Cam one of the most celebrated citizens of the city.

Dutch's mother was told on Monday morning by Beeson's head accountant to take an extra week's vacation until the excitement at her home had died down a little.

And on Wednesday, Curtin, the FBI man, called a meeting for Thursday morning at eleven o'clock. Surprisingly this meeting was not to be held at FBI headquarters or police headquarters but in Dr. Kilty's office at Fulmer Memorial Museum. And those present were to be, if at all possible, Dr. Kilty, Dutch Schildecker, Cam Osborn, Joe Barry, and Agent Curtin himself.

Cam took the day off from work. He wouldn't have missed the meeting for anything. He knew quite well that Curtin and Barry had been working to clear up the few loose ends of the fingertip mystery left dangling at the time of the Arabs' capture. And he suspected that they intended to explain it all to them at Thursday's meeting.

At eleven o'clock Dutch was already in Dr. Kilty's office with the curator when Cam and Joe Barry arrived together.

"Curtin not here yet?" Barry questioned.

"Not yet. Sit down," Dr. Kilty said.

"What's this meeting about?" Dutch asked Joe.

Barry shrugged, slanting a knowing smile at Dutch. "It's Curtin's meeting," he said. "He'll tell you."

Curtin arrived two minutes later. With him was a nattily dressed, birdlike little man who carried a briefcase under one arm.

"Sorry I'm late," Curtin apologized, "but Mr. Stone's plane was delayed." He proceeded to introduce them all to Stone, who calmly sat down in a chair with his briefcase across his knees.

Who's Stone? Dutch and Cam wondered. He had come in by air. Another FBI man? Curtin made no effort to enlighten them.

With a half smile he took the last vacant chair in the room. "All right," he began briskly. "Down to work." He looked at Dr. Kilty. "You're wondering why I called this meeting in your office?"

I am, yes.

"It's handier, that's all. Mr. Stone, will you please show Dr. Kilty the two exhibits?"

Without a word Stone unstrapped his briefcase and placed on Dr. Kilty's desk the five golden fingertips of Tut-ankh-amen and the flat gold necklace found in White Eyebrows' suitcase. Eagerly Dutch leaned forward to examine the necklace, which he hadn't seen before.

Dr. Kilty leaned forward, too, and gazed at the treasures, lost in an antiquarian's heaven. "Take a good look," Curtin said. "In your opinion, Dr. Kilty, are these genuine Egyptian antiquities? The real thing? You're an expert. We want your judgment. As a matter of form—and also to reassure Mr. Stone."

"These are indeed genuine," Dr. Kilty said without hesitation. "I'll guarantee it."

"Thank you." While Stone reached out and replaced the treasures in his briefcase, Curtin asked Barry, "Have you told them yet, Joe?"

Barry shook his head. "It's your baby."

"Good. Well, boys, you might be interested to know, then, that your two Arabs have made a statement. A confession, if you like. And signed it with their real names, Yakoub Ali and Selim Fayed."

Dutch stirred. "Jacob Allen and Salem Fay. Then they're real Arabs?"

"Absolutely. Legal papers and everything for a United States visit."

"For Arabs they spoke pretty good American," Cam said.

"Before they turned crooked they'd both been Cairo dragomen for years. Tourist guides, you know. Consorting every day of their lives with American tourists," Curtin explained, "they picked up a lot of Americanisms. That's what their statement says, anyway."

Dutch said, "Then they stole the stuff from the Cairo Museum's King Tut collection four years ago? Personally?"

"Yes. And you were right, Dutch, about those lists. Ali had one in his hatband. Fayed had one in the heel of his left shoe. And one was hidden under the lining of their plaid suitcase. All written in Arabic. And exactly what you guessed. A list of addresses and names; a keyed list of items they'd stolen from the Cairo Museum; and a list of various pieces of luggage, with notes on the exact location in each piece where they'd hidden an antiquity. Taken individually the lists made no sense. But together they formed a sweet little map to a lot of buried treasure! Mr. Stone. List number two, please. The translation."

Stone dug a paper out of his briefcase. Curtin handed it to Dr. Kilty. "Does that remind you of the list of stolen antiquities the Egyptian government circulated after the theft?"

Kilty, after one brief glance at the list, nodded emphatically. "I recognize the descriptions. They're of the same pieces. All very small, very compact, very suitable for concealment in small space. Do you want to compare this with the circulated list? I have one here."

"Already been done," Curtin said with satisfaction. "You're right about it." He handed the list back to Mr. Stone.

"What I want to know," Dutch said, "is how these thieves managed to hide the antiquities in the luggage in the first place."

"I couldn't figure that one either," Curtin smiled. "But I know now, thanks to their statement. They quit the guide racket and got jobs together in the luggage checkroom of the Nilotic Hotel in Cairo. They checked hundreds of pieces of luggage every day for hotel guests, many of them Americans. So they had access for varying lengths of time to plenty of American baggage. Hiding stolen antiquities in it seemed a nice, simple, foolproof way of getting the loot out of Egypt and into America without any trouble from Egyptian officials or American customs inspectors. They had the deal all figured out before they ever robbed the King Tut collection, so they stole only small, compact items that could be hidden in luggage—like the fingertips and Mrs. Cosgrove's necklace."

Dutch said, "Then you think my father checked one of his suitcases in the Nilotic Hotel checkroom in Cairo? And the Arabs sewed the gold fingertips into its hollow handle while they had it in their checkroom?"

"Sure. But your dad checked only one of his bags. The Arabs didn't know there was a second one until they stole the wrong one from you last week by mistake. They used the same system of concealment on Mrs. Cosgrove's car case—and a lot of others."

"How'd they know who the luggage belonged to?" Cam asked. "They had to know names and addresses of the owners or they could never recover their antiquities over here."

"Again they operated on a very simple plan. They sewed antiquities only into bags or trunks that had identification tags on them. You know, luggage tags that give the owner's name and address."

"Pretty slick," Dutch murmured grudgingly.

"It was slick, all right. First they robbed the museum in Cairo; then over a period of a year or so they concealed the stolen goods in American luggage and let unsuspecting Americans cart them off to America for them. They worked at their legitimate jobs in the checkroom until they saved enough money to afford a trip to America. Then they came over here to recover their treasure."

Dr. Kilty spoke up. "That's the most puzzling aspect of the affair to me, Mr. Curtin. Their antiquities, priceless as they are, couldn't be turned into cash like so much old gold at a pawn shop. The thieves would have to have a *market* lined up to realize any great amount of money on the loot."

Curtin grinned. "They did," he said. "They didn't miss any tricks at all. First thing they did when they landed in New York was to contact a Mr. Bazien Contoulis. He's a wealthy Greek who is also a collector of antiquities. They'd met him while guiding tourists in Cairo. He was one of their charges. Their statement claims that Contoulis offered to take the whole works off their hands, when found, for half a million dollars. No proof, of course, about that."

"Whee!" Cam exclaimed, impressed. "We were fooling with big money, Dutch!"

"Half a million is chicken feed for the things on that list," Dr. Kilty said, tapping his desk. "The Arabs were being taken."

Joe Barry laughed. "The poor innocent Arabs," he said. "My heart bleeds for them!"

Dutch said, "Mine doesn't!"

"Nor mine," Curtin agreed. "They'll get what's coming to them, don't worry."

Mr. Stone looked at his watch.

Curtin said, "You kids probably have a hundred questions you'd like answers to. But Mr. Stone has to catch a plane pretty soon. So let me give you a quick run-down of the Arabs' confession. Okay?"

Dutch thought: Mr. Stone just got here, and now he has to go away again. Who is he, anyway?

"Swell," said Cam.

Dutch said, "Does their statement answer the biggest mystery of all? Why they robbed *this* museum of *its* false fingertips?"

"It does."

Curtin lit a cigarette and blew smoke at the light fixture. Then he said, "After they made their deal with Contoulis, the Greek collector in New York, Ali and Fayed started out to collect their loot. Riverlawn happened to be the first stop for them. Your father's name and address was the first on their list, Dutch."

"Some honor!" Dutch said. "And Mrs. Cosgrove's was second."

"Right. So Ali and Fayed come to Riverlawn, register at a third-rate hotel, and settle down to learn what they can about one Oscar Schildecker, his home, his family, and his habits. They follow you around, watch your sister and mother, watch your house for a few days. They're being very careful. Then one afternoon when you're all busy elsewhere they make a straightforward attempt to burglarize your house. They think you're at track practice, Dutch, although you're really interviewing Dr. Kilty about this job that day. Your mother's at work as usual. Hilda's at her friend Rita's. So Ali, disguised by bushy black eyebrows and mustache, goes to your house, intending to pick the lock on the front door, mount to the attic or wherever you keep your luggage when not in use, pick up the suitcase described in his list, and calmly carry it away. But Hilda comes home unexpectedly early. She finds him on the front porch of your house."

"The secondhand dealer," Dutch said. "We figured that out."

"Yes. With admirable presence of mind, Ali switches plans, pretends he's a secondhand man wanting to buy old suitcases, hoping he can at least find out where the bag he wants is kept. When

Hilda didn't take the bait, he makes a strategic retreat to await a better opportunity.

"The better opportunity seems to have arrived the next day when your mother's at work, you're running in a track meet, and Hilda is watching it. This time Fayed, the taller Arab, impersonates a TV repairman, utilizing a ladder and truck stolen by Ali from a local painter. He wants his illegal entry into your attic window to look perfectly legitimate to any chance passerby. Ali waits outside in the truck."

"That's the day they ran the mile race early," Cam said, "and you went home for a nap, Dutch."

"Correct," Curtin said. "These poor guys were always being interrupted! When Fayed wakes Dutch up, he gets nervous and drops the corner of his master address list, which he has torn off for easy reference. He retreats. The Arabs decide to lay low until your suspicions, if any, Dutch, evaporate.

"They continue to keep tabs on you, though. You and Cam catch Fayed that same night checking on you through Cox's window, and you follow him home. But he's disguised with a toupee and pads in his mouth, so you think you're mistaken. Within the next few days you finish school, quit your job at Cox's, and begin work at Fulmer Museum. And Ali, following you to the museum one day, enters Egyptian Hall out of idle curiosity and inspects the exhibits. All at once he finds himself staring into a display case at what he takes to be the five fingernail covers of Pharaoh Tut-ankh-amen which he himself has stolen from the Cairo Museum!"

"But our fingertips were fake," Dutch protested.

"Sure. But he didn't know that then. He doesn't know much about antiquities, remember—only that they're valuable. He's a sneak thief, not an Egyptologist. And he knows he recognizes those fingertips. They're on his list; they're supposed to be hidden in a suitcase at your house. Put yourself in his place, Dutch. Those fingertips in your display case had to be the originals. Nothing else made sense. Anything else would be the wildest kind of coincidence, from his standpoint. For here's an obscure kind of antiquity—fingernail covers. They're exactly like the ones he stole in Cairo—five in number, a complete set for one hand. They're displayed in this particular museum, in this particular town where Oscar Schildecker, the first name on their "recovery" list, lives.

Schildecker even *works* in the museum now! Obviously Schildecker, or perhaps his father, has somehow discovered the fingertips concealed in the suitcase, recognized them as antiquities, and given or sold them to the museum. You see? Maybe the gift of the ancient fingertips to the museum has even been instrumental in getting young Schildecker, a mere schoolboy without adequate qualifications, his job there!"

"Well, thanks," Dutch said, raising his eyebrows at Dr. Kilty. "That explains their robbery of the museum, anyway."

"Yes. Ali reports to Fayed. They both inspect the display in your museum. They think the fingertips are genuine—what they've come to get from you. They decide to break into the museum and steal them. That's the only way they can recover the antiquities.

"They break in. They knock out the night watchman as planned. But then they're startled to find you, Dutch, working in the museum that night. That Schildecker pest again!" Curtin grinned at Dutch. "They dispose of you, too, by slugging you. They steal the fingertips. At Doheny's Hotel, in their room, they examine them carefully and find them to be false, mere copies. And not even very good ones. You could see the lead through the gilt paint in a good light, I understand?"

"To my shame," Dr. Kilty said. "I should have had them renewed long ago."

"Well," Curtin went on, putting out his cigarette in Dr. Kilty's alabaster ash tray, "now the police are involved. A crime has been committed. So the Arabs leave Riverlawn for a short time to wait for things to quiet down. They decide they might as well tackle the next assignment on their list—Mrs. Cosgrove's car case in Conawachie. Luckily it isn't far away.

"They hire a car, drive to Conawachie, put up at a down-at-the-heels motel near the inn. For three days they spy out the land, watching the Cosgroves and their house. On Sunday night, when they have made sure the Cosgroves are away, they enter the house and steal the car case. No trouble this time. They drive back into the woods to an abandoned road maintenance shed they have marked down previously as affording complete privacy…"

Cam burst in, "Boy, was it private! Like a cracker-box lost in an ocean of trees!"

"They examine the car case in the shed," Curtin continued. "They find the necklace they expect to find. And they spend the night there, sleeping in their car behind the shack."

"Why'd they do that?" Dutch asked.

"Because they'd already checked out of their motel before they stole the car case. Pretended they were leaving the lake, so they wouldn't be suspected if and when their burglary was discovered.

"Next day they drive back to Riverlawn. They resume their surveillance of your house and you, Dutch. They are hard put to it to dodge the attention of the police cruiser which is also keeping an eye on your house, at Joe Barry's orders."

"Say," said Dutch, "that reminds me, Joe. How come your police car wasn't on the job when they tied up Hilda?"

Joe blushed. "Those meatheads!" he muttered. "Curtin'll come to them."

Curtin laughed. "Your Arabs weren't lacking in a certain low cunning. They were pretty smooth workers. Anyway, imagine their joy and surprise on Saturday morning, while parked down the street from your house, to see your sister appear on your front porch with the very suitcase they've been trying to get from you! Before they can improvise any scheme for getting it, you and Cam and your girls come along, pick up the suitcase, and drive off.

"All they can think of to do is follow you. When you go to buy gas, Ali lets Fayed out of their car because you'd seen him before, and follows you into the gas station. He checks your brown suitcase at close range. Then he picks up Fayed again. Later, when they locate your car in front of Mrs. Cosgrove's place in Conawachie, they begin to suspect you know too much. They decide to waylay you. They settle on the old maintenance shed as the place to put you on ice for a while. While you're talking to Mrs. Cosgrove, Ali goes back to the village and buys a new padlock for the shed door.

"You know better than I do what happened after that. When the fingertips weren't in the suitcase they stole from you at Conawachie, they figured there had to be another suitcase just like it. And Hilda was forced to tell them where it was…"

"Come on, Joe," Dutch teased Sergeant Barry, "where were your cops when the Arabs got to Hilda?"

Curtin said, "I'll tell you. It hurts Joe's pride to talk about it. Joe's boys were lured away from your house by Fayed while Ali went in. Car seventeen was watching your house as instructed, parked across the street, when Fayed skidded up in the black Plymouth and reported witnessing an auto accident six blocks away, in which two children had been badly injured by a hit-run driver. He was terribly upset and said the police were needed there at once. Well, handling traffic accidents, and most especially hit-run cases, is part of the police job, so the cruiser took off at once, although it should have waited for radio instructions, of course. Anyway, it was gone long enough for Ali to get his information out of Hilda."

"My boys knew they'd been fooled when they found no evidence of an accident at the reported scene," Joe said in disgust, "and no injured kids. But that didn't help Hilda any. Because while they were out of their car investigating the nonexistent accident, somebody punctured all their tires. They were hung up there, and ashamed to report it."

"Fayed?" Cam asked.

"Who else? After reporting the fake accident, he followed them in his car, immobilized theirs, and scrammed back to pick up Ali."

Dutch said, "It could have happened to anybody. Sal was a smooth operator. We know."

Mr. Stone looked at his watch again.

"All right," Curtin concluded, "I can take a hint. I guess that's everything, boys. The Arabs' disguises were simple but effective in giving them a different appearance each time they were seen. But Fayed couldn't remember not to hunch his shoulders—and that's what put you on their trail, Dutch." Curtin paused. Then he said jokingly, "You kids would make great agents. You certainly did yourselves proud on this thing."

Cam flushed with pleasure. "We were kind of lucky, Mr. Curtin."

For no reason that the boys could see, Curtin laughed out loud at that. "Well," he said, drawling his words, "I guess maybe you're right, in a way. Especially Dutch."

Cam leaped to his friend's defense. "Dutch was a lot more than lucky! I was just a strong-arm man, but Dutch really figured this whole mess out!"

"That's what I mean," Curtin said, smiling. "But I'll let Mr. Stone explain it."

Startled, the boys switched their attention to the dapper little man with the briefcase. For the first time he smiled. And for the first time since entering the room he spoke.

"I'm afraid Mr. Curtin didn't tell you who I am," he began. "He wanted to surprise you, Dutch. I'm the New York representative of the insurance firm that insures the Tut-ankh-amen collection in the National Museum of Cairo. When those King Tut items were stolen four years ago by Ali and Fayed, our company paid off, of course. But the claim was naturally a very large one. And the insurance company therefore offered a reward for information leading either to the capture of the thieves or the recovery of the stolen antiquities, or both." Mr. Stone stopped and cleared his throat.

Dutch felt his heart beginning to thud against his ribs.

"You will realize, of course," Mr. Stone went on in his precise way, "that the three lists discovered in the possession of Ali and Fayed will now enable us to recover most, if not all, of the stolen antiquities presently secreted in the luggage of widely scattered Americans. You see that?"

"Sure," said Dutch. "You ought to get most of the stuff back."

"Exactly. I have been in touch with our home office, therefore, since I received news of your—ah—adventures, and I am authorized to present the promised reward, I am happy to say, to Mr. Oscar Schildecker, who has been largely instrumental in making possible the recovery of the antiquities and the consequent recovery of our insurance payment."

Dutch, speechless for a moment, said to Sergeant Barry, "So that's why you kept giving me credit in the newspaper stories! So I'd get the reward! You knew about it all the time, didn't you?"

"What's wrong with that?" Joe Barry said. "We just told the papers the truth. You deserve the reward if anyone does, Dutch."

"And Cam," Dutch said immediately. "Cam does."

"Fun and exercise," Cam said, laughing. "That's what I was in it for. Nothing else. I didn't contribute a thing to the actual solving of the mystery, Dutch. You owned the suitcase. You identified the tall Arab. You remembered the scrap of paper and found it. You suspected the connection with the Cairo thefts. And you knew all about Egyptian antiquities to begin with. I wouldn't know one if it came up and bit me! So don't give us the modest talk, old buddy! You're the white-haired boy around here. Face it like a man!"

Dutch stammered, "But Cam—"

"He's right, Dutch," Joe Barry cut in. "Mr. Stone has read the reports you and Cam dictated to us at headquarters. He's drawn his own conclusions from them, not the newspapers. And his conclusion is to give you the reward."

"Yes," Mr. Stone spoke up again. "And since my plane leaves in half an hour, I'd like to get this business disposed of, if you don't mind." He reached into his briefcase once again and withdrew a letter, typed on a sheet with a business letterhead. Mr. Stone stood up and said, formally, "Mr. Schildecker, my company asked me to deliver this letter to you personally. I now do so, with my company's warm thanks." He bowed and handed the letter to Dutch. Then he shook hands with him.

"Good work, Dutch," Curtin said, rising and giving Dutch no chance to do more than glance at the letter. "Thanks for the use of the hall, Dr. Kilty. And thanks for your professional endorsement of the genuineness of the antiquities. Joe, be seeing you again, soon I hope. Good-by, boys." He shook hands with Dutch and Cam, waved aside their thanks for his help. "Coming, Mr. Stone?" They left Dr. Kilty's office briskly.

"Well, well," Dr. Kilty said to Dutch a few moments later, "you look as if you'd suddenly stumbled on an unknown papyrus written by Khufu himself."

Dutch was staring at the letter in his hand. "I have, sir," he gulped. "Except you've got the wrong king! Midas would be more like it!" He looked with dazzled eyes first at Cam, then at Dr. Kilty whose mustache was tilted in a delighted smile. "This letter says Mr. Stone's company is sending the reward to my mother in trust for me. And you know what? The reward is twenty-five thousand dollars!"

Dr. Kilty was stricken into a deeply respectful silence at mention of such a munificent sum. But Cam, irrepressible, leaped three feet into the air and yelled, "Wow! May I be dipped in whale oil!" and gave a shrill, Tarzan-like cry, beating on his chest, so that every museum employee within earshot was startled half to death. Then Cam solemnly shook hands with Dutch. "You bloated financier!" he chortled. "You tycoon! You wealthy property owner! How about lending me a buck till payday?" He hugged Dutch in exuberant high spirits.

Dutch slowly stowed the letter in his pocket, shaking his head, still incredulous. Dr. Kilty touched the sleeve of his sports jacket. "What will you do with all that money, Dutch?" he asked gently. "As if I didn't know."

Dutch nodded. His eyes began to kindle. "Now," he said, "I'll be able to go to college! Now I can take care of mother and Hilda, too!" His voice rose. Then he faltered, "If I can get into any college with my grades, that is."

Dr. Kilty stood up. "Don't worry about that, Dutch," he advised. "You have another year at high school in which to bring up your grades. And my recommendation carries considerable weight at a certain college I know of. And Dutch"—Kilty reached out and shook his young assistant's hand with unaccustomed feeling—"it's a college where you can major in classical civilization!"

* * * *

Dutch and Cam left the museum together. It was almost lunchtime.

"Well," said Cam, hiding his delighted satisfaction at Dutch's windfall under a flippant manner, "how about that? You get knocked as cold as a mackerel and end up with twenty-five grand! You win a college education with a handful of false fingernails! That's doing it the hard way, son."

"Hard way is right. I guess I ought to be grateful to the Arabs."

"Huh-uh," Cam disagreed. They climbed into the jalopy parked in front of the museum. "If you want to feel grateful for something, how about the cool analytical brains that solved the mystery?"

"Our brains?"

"Ours. They won you your college education, not a couple of crooked camel drivers! They also," Cam went on with assumed smugness, "have made you and me, my friend, the darlings of Riverlawn girlhood! We're heroes. We're celebrities. There isn't a girl in town, I bet, who wouldn't give her eyeteeth for a date with either one of us."

Dutch nodded, polishing his nails ostentatiously on his chest. "Isn't it a dreadful bore to be famous, my good fellow?"

"Yeah." Cam started his car. "And speaking of dates, I heard some sad news last night. Kathy's folks are sending her to a private school in Massachusetts this fall."

"Hey! You mean Kathy's leaving Riverlawn High?"

"Yep. So I won't have a date for the football dance in October."

"Why not? You just said you could date any girl in town."

"You planning to take Janet?"

"Sure. Who else?"

"Well, as long as Kathy won't be here, maybe I'll try a new date."

"Anybody particular in mind?"

Cam looked sidelong at his friend. He felt good. He was steering the jalopy nonchalantly with one hand. "I think," he said with the air of a man reaching an important decision, "that I'll ask Hilda."

"Hilda!" Dutch stared at Cam as though he had suddenly sprouted bushy green eyebrows on his upper lip. "My sister? Are you nuts? She's just a kid, Cam! A freshman!"

"I know." Cam turned on his infectious grin. "But her brother is a very rich man, they tell me. And besides, Hilda thinks I'm gorgeous!"

Dutch laughed. "To tell you the truth, you aren't very gorgeous, pal. But you're one of the very finest Arab tacklers I know. So I'll think about letting you take Hilda to the dance."

"Gee," said Cam, "thanks, Dad. Coming from Oscar Schildecker, the great Dutch detective, that's something. So I'll think about it, too."

Happily they rode the jalopy down Main Street. "Where we going?" Dutch asked.

"To Cox's. For a hamburger. Okay?"

"Sure," said Dutch. "I'm starved. Are you?"

"No," Cam answered, laughing, "but I always think better when I'm eating!"

www.ingramcontent.com/pod-product-compliance
Lightning Source LLC
Chambersburg PA
CBHW020131180626
46810CB00004B/1503